THE VENUS ENIGMA

By
JOE GIBSON

I0616782

ARMCHAIR FICTION
PO Box 4369, Medford, Oregon   97501-0168

*The original text of this novel was first
published by Clark Publishing under the title:
"Down in the Misty Mountains"*

Armchair Edition, Copyright 2013, by Gregory J. Luce
All Rights Reserved

*For more information about Armchair Books and products, visit our
website at…*

www.armchairfiction.com

Or email us at…

armchairfiction@yahoo.com

MYSTERY IN THE MISTY MOUNTAINS OF VENUS

Kim Rothman was a seasoned space pirate, not afraid to take lives if necessary. Yet there was a purpose to his piracy— Earth's corporations had made it almost impossible to survive financially in the colonial settlements on Mars, Venus, and in the asteroid belt, charging astronomical prices for necessary provisions and machinery. But soon his piracy led to his chance meeting with Frances Freemont, a female survivor of his last raid. She then led him on a wild adventure back to Earth, and then back into space to the mysterious, rain-soaked planet of Venus, where tall mountain peaks were permanently hidden within the reddish-orange clouds that surrounded the planet. Hidden within these jagged mountains was an age-old secret that would soon shock all of mankind.

FOR A COMPLETE SECOND NOVEL, TURN TO PAGE 143

CAST OF CHARACTERS

KIM ROTHMAN
A typical space pirate, with two Maxim needle-guns strapped to his sides—and he was more than willing to use both of them.

FRAN FREEMONT
It's not often you get a chance to be saved by the very space pirate who blew your spaceship out from under you, but she did.

GROGOR DIMITRIOS
This eminent archeologist held space pirates in contempt, until he learned how valuable it was to have one on a space voyage.

MACNEARY
He was a fat, ruthless space pirate with no sense of morality. What he did have was a trio of sexy naked girls to protect him!

WU CHAO-TANG
This famed biochemist was willing to send those close to him on an interplanetary mission from which they might not return.

BARNEY KRUPA
The most powerful man on Ceresport. He could help you, or be your deadly enemy. The choice was yours.

YIN CHAO-TANG
Brother of Wu Chao-Tang. He wanted to save face in the eyes of his brother, but the price was far more than he bargained for.

It was a hundred years of progress; it was a hundred years of destruction; it was the Century of Great Dreams; it was the Century of Vast Illusions—thus, the era our early science-fiction writers depicted thud-and-blunderingly with Space Patrol and space pirates, ray-guns and rocket ships, bug-eyed monsters and beautiful maidens. It was all of that, and more!
It was the Twenty-Second Century—

Waldo Heinlein III
History and My Ancestors; 2354. A.D.

CHAPTER ONE
Riders of the Ring

PIRACY was a problem of vectors. The ship went this way, accelerated that way, through a gravitational drag another way, with a centrifugal force curving through there. Somewhere in that tri-dimensional pattern, jet-thrust was so much in such-and-such tubes according to mass-ratio and grav drag; grav plates adjusted so much according to stress curve and power available; power turbines were revved up according to fuel available for maximum output and possible future necessities.

A pirate couldn't be a fool.

Kim Rothman reminded himself of that fact as he watched the bright green spark glide across the radarscope.

That green spark was a space freighter, three months out from Lunaport, Earth, and bound for the New Holdings in the Jovian Moon-System. That freighter would be loaded with machinery, spare parts, mail and luxuries—the soap, coffee, and chocolate bar trade.

In the sleek, black hull of the pirate cruiser *Voodoo,* there were twenty-seven men from Marsport who wanted that space freighter. And Kim Rothman, seated at the broad control bank under the transparent blister, high on the cruiser's back, was supposed to get that freighter for them.

There were five billion people on Earth, and they were prosperous. They had plenty of skilled manpower and plenty of factories.

Hardier, pioneering individuals had settled the other planets. They had some factories inside their sealed, domed cities, and were self-sufficient so far as elementary necessities—air, water, food, and atomic fuel—were concerned. But, being so few and having to do so much just to stay alive on their alien worlds, they had neither the time nor the materials for manufacturing the luxury items, the comforts of civilization, the automatic machinery to make spare parts for their machines. These, they bought from Earth, in exchange for the minerals and produce grubbed out of the alien soil of their world.

And Earth charged high. Too high. The struggling, hard-working settlers just couldn't meet the prices demanded by Earth—demanded, of course, so that the people of Earth could live in the luxurious comfort to which they were accustomed.

So the settlers had simply been forced to stop buying.

And the Earth government, the United Nations, promptly revised the Articles of Space. Henceforth, interplanetary colonization could be conducted by large corporations on Earth, would be owned and operated by these corporations on Earth, and colonists would be employees of the corporations rather than free settlers. And the corporations would answer to the Earth government.

It was a mistake. There were civil uprisings in the domed cities of Mars, Venus, and Mercury.

The Earth government wouldn't back down. They placed an embargo on shipments to these worlds. They authorized the corporations to build, operate, and maintain their own spacecraft.

Until then, all spacecraft had been government-owned, operated by government-approved space crews. The spacemen had become an almost legendary breed of heroes, driving their ships across the black void to bring supplies to the far-flung settlements—often when such supplies were a matter of life-and-death.

But if the corporations owned spacecraft, the crews would have to follow the orders of the corporations. There would be no more swinging off course and forgetting your destination to answer the distress call of some colony of free settlers. Tradesmen lost money when that happened, but lives were often saved. The corporations wouldn't allow it—unless a distress call was relayed through their home offices on Earth and the news syndicates notified so they would get plenty of publicity for it.

The spacemen didn't like it.

Government-owned spacecraft began to disappear, complete with government-approved crews.

So Kim Rothman sat at the controls of his pirate cruiser *Voodoo,* carefully plotting his "run" on a space freighter five million miles away. The space freighter was a corporation ship, bound for the corporation-owned New Holdings in the Jovian Moon-System.

And behind Kim Rothman, in the crew's quarters of his cruiser, were twenty-seven men from Marsport who wanted to take over that space freighter and drive it back to Mars. The free settlers on Mars needed that cargo of machinery and spare parts. They couldn't get it from Earth. Not directly or legally.

Of such things, pirates are made.

KIM'S lean, strong hands leaped over the keyboard, his fingers deftly punching the proper keys. The pilot-computer clattered and yuk-yuked and twittered at his elbow. Bright little numbers leaped gloweringly onto a frosted slot. The data was integrated and signal lights flashed blue.

Target plotted; interception and coordination computed; ready in twelve minutes, fourteen seconds.

A female operative could have set up the pilot-computer much more easily and swiftly than he had. Women's reflexes were faster, which was why they were Second Officers aboard all larger spacecraft. But a man could coordinate the data to be fed the pilot-computer much easier and more comprehensively than a woman. Computers need cold, hard facts interwoven into a complete pattern. They would not compute intuition, which made men First Officers aboard larger spacecraft.

But both tasks were equally important in the operation of a ship. Both had to be done with precision and understanding; neither was valid without the other.

Kim was frankly wishing he had a female teammate on the *Voodoo*. The little cruiser wasn't meant for major space maneuvers; its control pit wasn't designed for a man-woman team. He knew he wouldn't have a really efficient pirate ship until he'd redesigned it—and had a girl who'd ride with him.

He locked the controls in their computed settings and flicked on the intercom screen. "Korsak," he called quietly.

Korsak's thin, pointed face loomed on the screen. He was a typically tall, lean Mars colonist, the son of a son of a Mars colonist. And he was a "government-approved" spaceman who wanted to pilot that freighter back to Mars.

"Hi, Rothman," he said. "About time, isn't it?"

Kim nodded casually. "I've already screened and set. Tell your men to prepare for four minutes' eight-gee acceleration."

Korsak scowled darkly. "Four *minutes?* That's kinda rough."

"I've shaved it as far as I can," Kim told him. "The gravplates will be on full fifty gees through the apex of the vector. Just pray we don't blow a circuit."

"They'll take evasive action." Korsak argued; he wasn't familiar with the piracy game. "You sure we can coordinate?"

"There's some risk," Kim admitted. "The computers allow for human decisions to a large extent, though. Better strap down—you've got eleven minutes…"

"Check." Korsak gave a curt nod and the screen went blank.

Kim surveyed the instruments, critically, then heaved a sigh of resignation and began to adjust his seat straps.

Dazzling fire burst from the tubes of the little cruiser. It slithered ahead, a slender, black needle in the dark emptiness of space.

Two million miles away, radarscopes registered on the control bridge of the freighter. Trajectories were computed; alarm bells clamored. A tall stout man studied the figures on the slots before him, made a grim decision, and spoke to his wife. The calm, efficient woman ran her fingers over the wide console keyboard. Red lights flashed in the crew-decks below as the freighter blasted its forward jet and heeled over. Then it cut back, crossed its former trajectory, its steel plates groaning with strain.

But the black ship followed. It closed in, slowly.

The freighter decelerated, all its forward jets spewing fire.

The black ship decelerated.

The freighter snapped off its forward jets; then its main jets opened up. It accelerated, shot forward.

The black ship accelerated.

Each action, in itself, meant little. The timing of each action meant everything. The pirate was a tiny green spark on the freighter's scopes; it was closing in on a long, shallow curve that dipped and swirled in gyrations that matched the freighter's exact maneuvers.

They were two thousand miles apart when the screens went up and the gun-crews manned their batteries.

Kim dragged himself back to a red-hazed consciousness and activated his own battery, six projectors mounted in a ball-turret on the cruiser's nose.

He held his fire until the freighter opened up. Two thin beams lanced out from the freighter's amidships; another shot from its nose.

He swerved the little cruiser and the beams broke off the curved shell of the force-screen. Only a direct hit would penetrate. But each dodging maneuver cost him speed. The freighter could hold him off past coordination limit unless he made a direct hit.

The freighter couldn't maneuver as easily. He capitalized on that weakness, set his fire control to utilize it, and pressed the red firing stud. Then he collapsed back in his seat, sweat pouring down the sagging muscles of his body. A sudden lurch left him weightless, sickened. Then acceleration clamped down again.

The beams lanced back and forth, automatically. They shattered off the invisible spheres of the force-screens. The ships closed in to a thousand miles; five hundred...

The final beam went exactly where Kim intended it. The cruiser was sweeping past the giant freighter, overshooting the coordination limit, when its beam shot back and crashed through the freighter's screen, hit the main jets and tore them from their mountings with a blinding flare of radiance. Then the cruiser decelerated sharply, retrograding back into the coordination limit. It floated serenely off the crippled freighter's right flank, level with the Solar Ecliptic.

Kim massaged the aching muscles of his face. His whole body tingled with needles of pain. He gulped air into his laboring lungs, blinked his tear-dimmed eyes, flexed his hands to get the knots of pain out of them. Then he flicked on the intercom.

"Pile out, Korsak!" he ordered hoarsely.

The colonist's thin face appeared on the screen, grinning wearily. "We are scrambling into our trappings now, Rothman. How does she look?"

Kim turned his head to stare out the transparent blister at the huge freighter, floating a few thousand yards away. Sunlight blazed along her torn, mangled tail. Her nose was in deep gloom, invisible against the blackness of space, save for the yellow lights glowing from her portholes.

"She's hulled, aft," Kim reported thoughtfully. "Power turbines are gone—you can't run beam projectors on battery juice—and her free air has escaped. You may have a stiff fight with her crew."

"We'll handle that," Korsak prophesied grimly. "How extensive is her damage—and are the cargo holds all right?"

"Cargo holds are intact," Kim replied. "But her main jets are gone beyond repair. You'll have to ride her back to Mars on auxiliary jets and set her on Phobos. She'd never make a planet-fall. If her turbines are shot, you may have to remain in spacesuits. It'll be a good six months' voyage, I'm afraid."

Korsak nodded. "We'll check when we get aboard. A beam kissed us, down here. You've got a leak in your belly plates under the turbine chamber; nothing serious. We've sealed the locks.

"I'll look at it," Kim said. "Get going."

The airlock swung open on the black hull and twenty-seven figures in bulky spacesuits jumped into space. Tiny rockets spouted flame from the tips of metal V-frames on their backs, and they floated off toward the giant, helpless hulk of the freighter.

Kim watched them go with a dull, numbing relief. His job was done. He had five thousand credits stuffed into the belt around his waist. He only waited to see that the final provision of his contract was carried out.

The tiny, ant-like figures disappeared in the gloom of the freighter's hull. The blue flares of cutting torches appeared.

Kim loosened his seat straps, unzipped the top of his spacesuit, and fished his cigarettes out of his jacket pocket. He puffed a cigarette alight, crossed his arms over his thickly padded chest, and waited.

Twenty minutes later, a small lifeboat roared out of its launching slot in the freighter's hull. He caught a brief glimpse of the space-suited freighter-crew under the transparent shell of the little craft; then it shot off into the star-sprinkled emptiness.

The communications light flashed on; before him. He tuned the intercom screen and flicked it on.

Korsak gave him a lopsided grin through the thick quartzite of a fishbowl helmet. "We're in, Rothman..."

"Everything check?" Kim asked brusquely.

Korsak nodded. "Killed two men and a woman—gun crew-members. They put up a fight while the others barricaded themselves on the control bridge. We lost four men before we got 'em. We evacuated nine people, all the survivors, in that boat. They've got enough fuel and provisions to raise Ceres."

"I'll check when I reach Ceres," Kim promised.

Korsak chuckled, "I know you will! Our agent will contact you there, if we've any more jobs lined up."

"Have a good voyage," Kim muttered, and flicked off the screen.

He crawled out of his seat and climbed wearily down the ladder—well to the cruiser's main salon. His gaze went yearningly to the liquor cabinet, set flush in the comfortable, luxurious wall furnishings, then he swung away and stamped heavily aft. He reached up with a gloved hand and rocked the fishbowl helmet forward, over his head.

He had to repair that leak, first. Then he had a three-week's cruise to Ceres. Alone. And there weren't any new magazines and telerecordings in the small library to help while away that time. He couldn't even open up with the ship's radio and talk to the far-flung Space Communications stations—they'd take a reading of his transmitter and vector him back to the spot that the freighter was attacked. Then the Space Fleet would be alerted. They'd come barreling out to intercept him.

The so-called Space Fleet was more precisely the "Earth Fleet," organized to stop these pirate raids on the ships and outposts of the Earth corporations.

The little *Voodoo* would be no match for any one of their huge dreadnoughts. He was alone. Completely alone. If he was in trouble, he couldn't call for help. There was no help for a pirate...no help for a pirate...

Blast it, he needed a pardner!

CERESPORT was a domed frontier outpost on the Asteroid Belt—the Ring, as it was called in spacemen's parlance. There was the giant dome and a flat, rocky plain, nothing more. The plain was usually littered with the small, blackened cruisers of asteroid prospectors and mining crews, plus the occasional fat Cigar of a supply freighter. Space Fleet dreadnoughts dropped in now and then, eyeing the little, nondescript ships with hostile suspicion.

For good reason, of course; not a few of Ceresport's "prospectors" were space pirates.

It was a wild, free outpost. Its habitués, men, women, and children, were a tough breed and knew it. Everyone over twelve years of age carried a holstered Maxim needle-gun. Like any free society far from the lawful restraint of civilization, it bred a few individuals who used their complete freedom to steal from others. Claim jumping was an everyday occurrence; murder averaged twice a week.

These people were intelligent. No illiterate could handle a spacecraft in the jumbled rock of the Ring. But honor and crime have no respect for technical training. Criminals are intelligent, too.

Kim brought the *Voodoo* sizzling in over the field, fire streaking from the forward jets. The little ship slowed to a halt above a cleared area and settled gently to the rock on her humming gravs. His spacesuited figure leaped down from the airlock and went skipping across the field, almost weightless in the planetoid's faint gravity.

He spotted the lifeboat near the dome, nodded his satisfaction, and bounded up to the city's giant entrance locks. He opened the outer portal and let himself in, sealed it and released air into the chamber. The inner portal opened automatically. He stepped through, feeling the underground grav-plates drag him down with normal one-gee, and walked over to the Locker Room.

His spacesuit went into a rented locker, and he buckled a pair of .003 mm. Maxim guns about his thighs and strolled on into the city.

He was a tall, lean figure in jacket and shorts. His hair was brown, his eyes gray, his features well formed but lacking any striking quality of handsomeness. He wasn't muscular, was neither fat nor thin. His appearance was of the common, ordinary kind that people passed up without so much as a glance.

He had come to appreciate that since assuming his pirate role. He noticed it, happily, as he strolled along the broad corridors past the solid doorways of residence apartments and the bright windows of shops, restaurants, and taverns. There were three thousand people in Ceresport, plus a usual five or six thousand transients. His presence would go unheralded.

He rode the escalators to Level Nine, the observation level under the transparent roof at the very top of the giant dome. Level Nine was famous throughout the Ring. It was the spacemen's meeting-place, a broad, circular chamber with an oval bar and scores of small, upholstered booths. Robot waiters scurried about on silent rollers, serving the men and women who sprawled in the booths, conversing in a loud murmur of sound while the stars glared down coldly from above.

Barney Gruka, the fat, ponderous proprietor of Level Nine, was stationed at his usual place in the small, glass-enclosed booth behind the entrance. His chill blue gaze flickered over Kim as the young spaceman approached the booth, but his puffy features showed no hint of recognition. Kim was acquainted with that ruse. He pushed aside the glass panel and eased himself into the seat across from Barney. The proprietor's fat hands played over the keyboard in the tabletop and a cool, iced drink plopped from a wall slot at Kim's elbow. The glass panel slid itself closed, shutting out the rumble of voices.

"Welcome back, Rothman," Barney greeted softly. His face retained its plump, smooth blankness. Nothing moved but the chill eyes and the fat lower lip.

Kim gazed at him musingly. There had never been a killing in Level Nine. No man had ever pulled a Maxim gun without having one of Barney's little steel robots grab him, shattering his gun-hand. And few things were said or even hinted at in Level Nine without Barney knowing about it. In fact, there were few people in Ceresport whose life histories weren't completely documented in the memory-files of the fat man's cunning brain—few people wandering along the Ring, itself, that he didn't at least know about.

"Anyone looking for me, Barney?" Kim asked gently.

The chill gaze touched him, briefly, and the lower lip stuck out in a faint pout. "Pay me," Barney demanded in his soft, liquid voice. "You know the rates."

Kim slipped a few credit notes out of his belt and laid them on the table, his palm covering them.

"No one is looking for Kim Rothman," Barney complied readily. "The survivors of the *Walrus*, a corporation freighter, are looking for the pirate who jumped them on the Earth-Jupiter run, three weeks ago. There are nine of them; three were killed when the pirates boarded the *Walrus*. Howard Tucker is First Officer."

Kim slid the credits across the table. They vanished up a loose sleeve in Barney's green satin tunic.

"One of the men killed was an investigator for the Biochemical Research Department," Barney remarked absently. "The corporations paid the Earth government to send him out for an investigation of the New Holdings on Ganymede. Some sort of corrosive agent is attacking the metal of their domes."

Kim tasted his drink, cautiously. The pungent liquor stung his nostrils. He set it down. "The Earth government isn't going to like having their investigator knocked off. The Space Fleet will probably put a price on that pirate's head."

"That is a minor detail," Barney scoffed, his eyes constantly shifting, watching. "Space is an interesting place, Rothman. It has some interesting tales. Some men change when they get out here."

"This investigator changed?"

"There is a girl, a Miss Frances Freemont, who was assigned as the investigator's assistant," Barney explained. "She's one of the survivors. She says her investigator turned wolf in space, tried to attack her in her stateroom, had to have some sense beaten into him by some of the ship's crew. She's not sorry she won't be his assistant, now."

Kim grimaced wryly. "That could be true or false. Maybe she claimed she was attacked, hoping the dumb investigator would fire her from the job on Callisto. Maybe she wanted to be a camp woman—"

"Possibly," Barney admitted. "She hasn't been flirtatious here, though. And she has a Second Officer's certificate."

Kim took out his cigarettes, rose, and pushed the glass panel open. "Thanks," he said. "I'll drop by again sometime." Stepping out of the booth, he poked a cigarette between his lips and strolled toward the long, oval bar.

Some men thought Barney Gruka knew too much. A number of men had tried to remove him. No one had succeeded nor lived to tell about it. Kim felt a keen irritation at the fat proprietor's shrewd knowledge, but he had no intention of challenging it. Barney also kept his mouth shut, when he was paid enough. Kim paid him enough.

A robot bartender brought Kim the mild, tasteful liquor he ordered. He filled his glass and hooked his elbows solidly on the bar. Men and women jostled and talked around him. Most of them wore jackets and shorts, though a few men wore trousers and a few women wore skirts. All of them wore guns. They were husky, well-formed people with light tan complexions. A few exceptions were negroes and whites, the two "vanishing races" of Earth. There were several seven-foot, dark-skinned sons of Mars, a couple of pinkish-white sons of Venus. Some men were close-shaven, some women's hair fell to their hips. There was one family of baldies, a man-and-wife team who preferred to shave their heads. It was a matter of personal preference.

Kim studied them all, savored their talk. The words were a fantastic mixture of languages, though most of them spoke the spacemen's form of pidgin English with familiar phrases, and expressions of French, German, Cantonese, Nipponese, Spanish, and Russian thrown in. He recognized the speech of one husky male-female team as Mongolian.

His elbow was nudged gently. He turned to find a grinning, curvaceous girl standing beside him. "Come over to my booth and let's talk," she invited musically.

Kim shook his head. "I'm not in the mood for happy talk," he replied gravely.

The girl's eyes narrowed and her slender hand dropped to the gun on her hip. She surveyed him slowly from head to foot, then turned and stalked off, hips wriggling sinuously. The holstered gun slapped against her leg.

Kim shrugged and turned back to his drink. He had no liking either for alcohol or women, the two chief diversions offered at any frontier outpost. Some spacemen went in for both as soon as they hit a port. Some spacewomen teamed with men and lived with them during voyages, then went seeking variety as soon as they hit port and eventually shipped out with another man. Some spacemen and women worked as teams and lived strictly apart on voyages. Some married and stayed together as teams, even raising their children aboard ship. Moral integrity, or the lack of it, had little bearing on how well they did their jobs.

It was a phenomenon of human nature that often intrigued him, drawing his thoughts off into a wandering tangent as was the usual habit of a man who spent long weeks alone. Kim shook his head, grinning to himself, and sipped his drink. He had other things to think about.

First, the *Voodoo* had to be fueled and provisioned, worn-out parts replaced and mechanisms inspected and overhauled. Second, he had to meet the agent from Marsport who, according to Barney, obviously had not arrived yet. And third—

Third, he had to find a teammate.

Kim scowled, perplexedly. He knew himself to be an admirer of moral integrity. His social prejudice would never quite allow him to have complete trust in a female teammate who practiced sex as a means of purely personal enjoyment. To him, such promiscuity was too emotionally selfish of either man or woman. He couldn't respect such an individual. He wouldn't want to share weeks and months with a woman like that.

His teammate would have to appreciate moral values. At the same time, she would have to agree with the principles that made him a pirate to the extent of becoming a pirate, herself.

Such a girl was not easily found. Most of them became wives of spacemen shortly after graduating from the Space Academy.

The ideal teammate would be a girl who agreed to join him, was attracted to him, and eventually mated with him. There were no marriages for pirates. His name and the *Voodoo's* former name were down on the Earth government's lists as a deserter; capture meant life imprisonment. It would have to be a common-law marriage.

He didn't have one chance in a million of finding such a girl in the Ring. Spacewomen who accepted commissions out here, where men and women rode the asteroids alone, were not those who wanted respect and decent teammates.

"You're sure deep in thought," a new voice growled at his elbow.

Kim turned and grinned at a tall, grizzled spaceman. "Kind of hard to lose the habit when you're just in from space, lone voyage," he admitted, moving aside to give the stranger room at the bar.

"My name's Ackerman," the spaceman said, running a nervous hand through his graying hair. "That must've been you that came sizzling over the dome, half an hour ago."

Kim nodded. "I just sold out a rich claim to a mining outfit," he lied pleasantly. "Guess I'll rest up a few days or a week, maybe, and strike out again."

Ackerman pressed the bar-stud, signaling the robot-bartender. "I got a pitchblende claim out on Dead Pete. Come in for supplies day before yesterday. Guess I'll go back when my pockets are empty." He chuckled dryly and ordered a stiff shot of Venusian rum from the bartender, which blinked its nose-light in acknowledgement.

"Does a man good to get in, once in a while," he continued, turning back to Kim. "Eat some good food, 'stead of concentrates. Have a few drinks. Associate with other people." His thoughtful brown gaze studied Kim's features, speculatively. "If my claim was rich enough to sell out for mining, I'd fuel up and head back to Earth," he added, then hastily amended, "I mean no insults."

Kim stilled the hand that had started toward his hip, put it back on the bar. "My name's Rothman," he replied easily.

Ackerman nodded. "Glad to meet you. Saw you brush off the buxom babe, a few minutes ago. She's been trying every lone guy in the joint."

"You brushed her off, too?" Kim asked guardedly.

"I turned and walked off. My back itched, though—I'm glad they don't allow killings in Level Nine." Ackerman picked up his drink as the robot slid it before him. "I've a few friends here in Ceresport," he added, sipping his drink. "There's a family I can always stay with when I'm here. It's nice to be welcome someplace, toddle some youngsters on your knee and tell 'em space tales."

Kim frowned in faint irritation. This, he knew, was another result of loneliness with some men: when they got back among their own kind, they talked and talked and talked to anyone who'd listen to them.

He started to pick up his drink and move away when Ackerman asked, suddenly, "You wouldn't consider a run back to Earth?"

Kim started visibly. "What makes you ask that?" he demanded.

Ackerman was giving him the thoughtful stare again. "There's a young lady here named Fran Freemont," the grizzled spaceman said quietly. "She's looking for passage back to Earth. The supply ship isn't due out for another three months." He set his drink on the bar and faced Kim, squarely. "I think you're a man she could trust, Rothman..."

Kim felt a tight constriction in his throat. "Thanks," he said gruffly. "But it just happens I'm not going back to Earth."

CHAPTER TWO
The Girl From Earth

HE spent the first three days provisioning and doing maintenance on the *Voodoo*. He slept on the ship, ate his meals at the city restaurants, and spent his spare time wandering around the broad corridors. He spent an afternoon with Ackerman at the apartment of the family the spaceman knew, playing poker for small stakes. He watched the spaceport field closely, noting the arrival and departure of each craft.

The agent from Marsport still hadn't arrived.

He was having dinner in the Black Vein Restaurant on Level Four when a small, skinny man walked over and slipped into the booth across from him. He looked up, blankly querulous.

"Barney says someone is looking for passage to Earth," the little man said, without introduction.

"So she finally want to Barney, huh?" Kim smiled grimly.

"She can't make passage out," the little man said. "There's no ships leaving. She'll pay a thousand credits to get back to Earth, no questions asked."

Kim's brows went up. "That gal's kinda anxious."

"Message center got an ether-gram, yesterday." The little man was brimful of information. "She's wanted for a special expedition to Venus—something about her being an authority on Venusian mammals. She'll get a promotion if she can make it."

Kim forked hunks of steak into his mouth and chewed thoughtfully. "Wha'd Barney say?" he mumbled.

"Nothing. You're here, your contact hasn't shown up. Barney wants ten percent."

"Does he, now?" Kim considered, musingly. Nine hundred credits was still a nice profit for a run to Earth. It was all downhill, toward the Sun's attraction. He could slip in to Earth, if he had a place to hide the *Voodoo*.

The little man seemed to read his thoughts. "She says she knows where a deserter ship could be hidden," he said. "Her family's some sort of well-to-do scientist outfit, has an estate in the Mongolian plateau country."

"Tell Barney I'll see her," Kim said decisively.

The little man slid out of the booth and walked away.

Kim finished his meal and returned to his ship. He pulled off his spacesuit in the airlock and clamped it to the wall, then strolled on into the main salon.

"Hello," the girl's voice said.

He whirled, yanking out his guns.

She was sitting in the low seat in the corner of the salon. Her figure was small, neatly rounded, attractive. She wore a two-piece garment of rich blue, embroidered in silver, a sort of scant bolero jacket and short, swinging skirt. It was rakish, fashionable, civilized; its color matched her eyes, which widened as she stared into the muzzle coils of his guns.

Kim lowered his guns and scrutinized her, critically. Her hair was light brown, close-cropped, and waved. Her skin was pale, like new ivory, her lips small and petulant red. Her fingernails were manicured. Her shapely knees were crossed, her legs smooth and firm. She did a lot more primping than most spacewomen, dressed for appearance rather than comfort or utility, and didn't wear a gun.

"You're Fran Freemont," he stated flatly.

She folded her hands on her knees, nervously, and tried to appear calm. "Is it that obvious?" she asked.

"I'm afraid it is." Kim nodded, holstering his guns. "You look like a well-paid government job with the Biochemical Research Department. How did you get out here?"

"I rented a spacesuit and came out."

He arched a critical brow. "In that outfit? In a *spacesuit?*"

"It doesn't wrinkle," she replied evenly. Somehow, she seemed more sure of herself, then. "After I talked to Mr. Gruka in Level Nine, I watched him and followed the man he sent to talk to you. So I knew you were the man I wanted to see."

"Why do it that way?" Kim asked, puzzled.

"I was afraid you might say no," she explained cryptically. Her gaze was steady, unflinching.

"If I had, nothing you could do would change it," Kim said, taking out his cigarettes.

She shrugged indifferently. "I didn't know that. But if you said yes, there's something else."

Kim puffed a cigarette alight. "What?" he demanded.

"I'll pay you one thousand credits and we'll take off for Earth immediately," she said in her cool, even tones. "Then you won't have to pay Mr. Gruka any percentage."

Kim grinned sourly. "Neat," he said. "But first, you'll go back and pay Barney Gruka one hundred credits."

Fran Freemont looked vaguely surprised. "Well..." she exclaimed. "There *is* honor among thieves!"

Kim felt deeply grateful that she hadn't said pirates. "Among a few of us, let's say," he corrected mildly. "And somehow, we few seem to have an ability to stay alive longer than the others. Also, it's easier to do business."

Her lips pressed together in faint irritation. "Couldn't you pay Mr. Gruka next time you came to Ceresport?"

"Barney would hardly appreciate that attitude," Kim chided, grinning. "I may be dead before I ever get back to Ceresport."

She rose with a sigh of resignation. "All right, then. I suppose I'll just have to climb into my spacesuit and go back to pay him."

Kim nodded mockingly. "I suppose you will."

He stood in the control pit, topside, and watched her bulky, spacesuited form move awkwardly back across the field. There was a dim shadow of emotion somewhere back in his mind that had prompted him to take her proposition. Otherwise, he hadn't had any intention of making a trip to Earth. He frowned, trying to puzzle it out.

Maybe it was just the rakehell humor of the deal, pirating an Earth corporation space freighter, then taking one of the freighter's survivors back to Earth and flaunting himself under Earth's very nose! Spitting in the devil's left green eye, so to speak. Buckling a swash...

Well, he was a pirate, wasn't he? The trouble was, *how did she know which ship was his?*

The answer came with a faint, muffled hammering on the *Voodoo's* hull, below.

Kim descended the ladder-well and went back to the airlock chamber. He pressed the stud that flashed the green "welcome" light outside and peered through the porthole as three shadowy, spacesuited figures shuffled into the lock. Air hissed from the valves as they closed the outer portal behind them, then the inner portal swung aside and they stepped in to face him.

The first visitor flung back his helmet with a sigh of relief. "Good evening, Mr. Rothman," he said pleasantly.

He was a small, sandy-haired man with a pink-cheeked face and a little mustache. Very dapper. The two men behind him were big, wide, husky, and ugly as sin.

"You know me and I don't know you," Kim replied casually. "And what makes it so good?"

"One thing makes it a very charming evening," the sandy-haired man said, smiling. He had a sneaky smile, Kim thought. "The one thing," he explained patiently, "is that no one was forced to have any accidents. It all worked out very well, and my name is Ted Brown."

"Well, Mr. Brown," Kim said, through his most charming smile, "I would ask you and Bill Smith and John Jones, here, to come in and have a drink—only, people who talk about accidents make me nervous."

Mr. Brown nodded amicably. "Quite understandable, Mr. Rothman. I shall be more specific. The young lady who asked the identity of your ship was, I believe, interested in making a deal with you. She desires to return to Earth, which is very commendable except that we have no desire to see you journey to Earth."

"Why not, please?" Kim inquired gently.

"Because," said Mr. Brown, placing his gloved fingertips together, "we have a deal which we wish to make with you, Mr. Rothman."

Kim stared at the two men behind Mr. Brown, at the way their gloved hands rested on the butts of their Maxim pistols. "Do come to the point, Mr. Brown," he muttered.

"Precisely." Mr. Brown nodded. "I, sir, am here as a representative of the Earth corporations which have interests in the New Holdings of the Jovian Moon-System."

Kim switched his stare back to the sandy-haired man. "You're *what?*" he gasped.

Brown laughed shyly. "Let me finish, sir. As you probably know, we have lost considerable money in the New Holdings. Our space freighters are being raided, our employees are in a bad humor, and our stocks are taking a terrible beating—this, in spite of all the Space Fleet can do to keep down these pirates, mind you..."

Kim's mouth gaped open. He couldn't believe it. They weren't—

But they were.

"It is my purpose," said Brown smiling, "to contract a number of space pirates to raid the supply ships that trade at the free ports of Mars and Venus, Mr. Rothman, and sell their loot to us. Fight fire with fire, you understand."

Kim controlled his features with an effort. "What makes you think I'd be interested?" he asked dryly.

"Both you and this ship are on the Earth government's deserter list," Brown replied smugly. "Please, Mr. Rothman, let's not quibble. We shall be proud to consider your immediate services, sir."

"Suppose I'm *not* interested?" Kim asked.

Brown's pale blue eyes became frosty. "We should be deeply disappointed. In fact, I might tell you that if Miss Freemont hadn't left here, after obviously having you refuse her proposition, we should never have allowed this ship to leave Ceres. Our ship is just twenty yards away, Mr. Rothman, and we had our batteries trained on you every second."

"In short, if I refuse—"

"It will be fatal."

Kim's first shot holed the big, wide, ugly man on the right. His second shot caught the big, wide, ugly man on the left, just as that worthy gentleman got his gun free. Both gentlemen were quite instantly dead, rendering the airlock chamber somewhat messy.

Mr. Brown skipped backward with a small, gurgling scream. Kim felt utter loathing, rather than anger, as he blew the small man's pale blue eyes and sandy hair into a bloody smear on the aft bulkhead.

Kim unbuckled his guns and donned his spacesuit. There was a cold lump in his stomach and his limbs felt dead. He dragged the three corpses into the airlock, closed the inner portal, pumped the air out, and opened the outer portal.

The huge, balloon-shaped bulk of Barney Gruka, in spacesuit, stood in the cold starlight outside, staring up at him.

"You all right?" Barney asked, through the helmet phones.

"Well as can be expected," Kim answered.

Barney gave a moist, whistling sigh. "I was afraid I hadn't figured out their game in time—"

"You didn't," Kim interrupted mildly. "Help me unload 'em."

Barney stood rooted to the spot as Kim stooped, lifted Mr. Brown's body, and heaved it forward out the airlock door. The body flipped over and tumbled onto the barren rock like a limp sack.

"I'll get somebody to bury 'em," Barney said softly.

IT TOOK ten weeks to reach Earth. Two and a half months in which the *Voodoo* seemed to be standing still in the black emptiness of the Universe. Human perspective narrowed down and a ship became a world on such long trips.

Kim had the airlock chamber mopped down and scrubbed before the girl returned from the Ceresport dome. He was in the salon mixing drinks when she entered, informing him that her luggage was already aboard and, if he didn't mind, she was anxious to leave that godforsaken space-hole behind her. Fran Freemont hardly appreciated Ceres.

The harsh sunlight was just splattering the tips of the jagged rock hills when they lifted. Kim locked the controls in their automatic settings and there was nothing more to that; he merely had to take an occasional star reading to check the computed course and inspect the ship's mechanisms regularly to see that they functioned.

He moved his belongings out of the small main stateroom and left it to Fran, moving into the large crew's quarters amidships. He didn't want her to notice the deck-fittings where twenty-seven acceleration couches had been mounted—he'd had the couches removed at Ceresport— because she just might reach the proper conclusions.

Fran Freemont was far from being naive. He learned that as they spent long hours in the control pit. He sprawled in his seat before the broad bank, watching the instrument readings for signs of trouble, and she perched behind him with her slim legs swinging over the edge of the ladder-well. There were breathless moments when red signal-lights flashed and the screen flicked on automatically, sights of awesome beauty as meteorite swarms crept out of the blackness and rained against the screen in brilliant splashes of fire. Once, the radarscope flashed into life and a fist-sized meteorite made a bright green streak across it.

Their conversations began in halting monosyllables, then gradually grew from habit. Fran was the daughter of an agricultural chemist who did government research on Venus; she was born in Venusport, grew up on Earth. Her mother's family was the famous Chao-Tang, renowned for the geological findings of the three Chao-Tang brothers, her uncles. It was a traditional family of scholars and scientists in the Orient. Fran held out her arm, showing him her ivory skin, with a faint smile; she told him of her childhood, a comfortable, happy childhood in her parents' small home, and of breath-taking visits to the wealthy Chao-Tang estate. Her young astuteness was duly noted and she was well educated, graduating from the Space Academy and earning her Master's degree in biochemistry at the University of Prague.

Her blithe narration loosened Kim's reluctant tongue. He told of his parents, prospectors of the Asteroid Belt who migrated from Earth's Middle East; he was born in their small cruiser, grew up on the Ring. They had paid his passage to Lunaport, where he graduated from the Space Academy, and he returned to establish a shuttle-supply service to the prospectors' diggings and mining claims around the Ring. That was before the Earth government revised the Articles of Space.

His parents had gone out on a prospecting jaunt, once, and had never returned.

Fran lapsed into sorrowful silence whenever Kim spoke of the hardships of his youth—the food concentrates, the stale tanked water, the necessity of a young boy learning the mechanical functions and maintenance of a spacecraft—and she didn't share his laughter as he related his first sight of Lunaport, when he was fifteen, and his first television show, his first pair of long pants, his first volleyball game. Kim noticed her silence and ceased talking about himself; he reverted to questioning, drawing her out of her own shell.

Her father's work and her faint memories of Venusport had prompted her to take up biochemistry—Venus was a hothouse planet of seething, ferocious life. "That's why I simply *had* to get back to Earth!" she exclaimed happily, as they were seated at dinner one late watch.

Kim's gaze drank in the beauty of her small, oval face in the soft light of the salon. "All I heard was that they had some special expedition lined up for Venus," he admitted, between mouthfuls. It was a relief that his normal, wolfish eating habits no longer bothered her. "And if you could make it," he went on, "they'd give you a promotion."

"Oh, that's nothing as far as I'm concerned," she refuted gaily. "The important thing is this—would you believe it—they've *discovered intelligent life on Venus...*"

"Huh?" Kim straightened up in surprise.

"The old legends about the Venusians are *true,*" she insisted, her eyes shining with enthusiasm.

Kim managed to withhold a grin. "There are quite a number of such legends, aren't there?" he asked chidingly, "What about the Martians who're supposed to live in the sands of the deserts and only dig their way out at night? And I seem to recall a number of old prospectors' tales of an asteroid where the rocks roll themselves around and talk to each other—"

"This is *not* an old prospector's tale," she denied somewhat vehemently.

"It was considered to be just a fantastic story, when they first heard about it," Fran explained grimly. "That was fifteen years ago—no, twenty. Anyway, an old-time reptile hunter came stumbling into Venusport one day, half-dead with fungus fever. Before he died, he told about finding a tribe of frog-like savages up on the slopes of the Misty Mountains. A couple of hunters followed his trail back and found some tracks of strange, unknown creatures—like bear tracks, their report said, only Venus hasn't any bears...

"Anyway, nobody really believed it, but Biochemical Research happened to have a teleologist named Thompson at Venusport."

"What's a teleologist?" Kim interjected.

"They specialize in organic adaptations. I've specialized in zoology the past few years, more so than biochemistry—especially mammalogy. Anyway, this Thompson set out to see what he could find. The tracks were washed away by then, of course, but—"

"But Thompson never returned..."

"Biochemical Research immediately sent out other investigators to organize search-parties for Thompson, and of course, to see what *they* could find. But none of them ever found anything. Not a trace."

"So?"

Fran gave him a wide-eyed, triumphant smile. "So the Department sent me an ether-gram after I notified them I was safe on Ceres. They asked me to return to Earth, if I could arrange passage, because they wanted me on the new expedition being outfitted for Venus.

"And they said one other thing. I knew what it meant, instantly. They said: 'Thompson came back.'"

CHAPTER THREE
The Man From Space

GRADUALLY, their relationship grew less formal. Before the breakfast hour, Fran was usually locked in her stateroom; then, accidentally, she left the door standing open. As he was passing in the corridor, Kim glimpsed her sitting before the mirror in silken pajama shorts and jacket. Her face was smeared with creamy paste and her hair was twisted tautly into pin-curlers. Kim leaned weakly against the doorjamb, laughing. But from then on, the door was left open.

She cut his hair and let him cut hers—with the clipper-dome it was easy—and alternated watches with him in the control pit. She borrowed an old pair of his shorts and jacket, and joined him in crawling through the ship's steel intestines, inspecting and repairing, cleaning and oiling. She assumed the role of ship's cook after he showed her a few culinary tricks with food concentrates. She helped him polish the quartzite ports and vacuum down the bunks and upholstery. She repainted the ship's galley.

They had hardly reached the halfway mark in their trajectory when she asked to use the ship's radio. Kim refused flatly.

They were seated in the control pit—Kim was in the seat and she had climbed down into his lap—when she hinted about it again.

She merely wanted to contact the Biochemical Research Department at Lunaport and tell them she was coming—and find out more about the expedition.

"You should've taken care of that before we left Ceres," Kim replied grimly. "The answer is no—the radio stays locked."

A broadcast to Lunaport, he knew, would be as good as calling the Space Fleet and telling them he was on his way. All spacecraft ran on schedules registered with Earth—except deserter craft, like the *Voodoo*. Space Communications at Lunaport would take a vector reading on his transmitter as a matter of routine. Then they'd notify the Space Fleet. Any ship on an unscheduled course was, naturally, a deserter.

Fran tried pouting for about five seconds. It didn't work. Then, she treated him coolly. Their talk lapsed back into monosyllables. That didn't work, either, and Kim knew she was beginning to wonder.

He knew, too, when she stopped wondering. It was when he entered the turbine chamber on a routine inspection and found the film of grease scrubbed off the steel deck around the shiny, new stress-beam. He had installed the stress-beam at Ceresport.

And where the oil-film was scrubbed away, there was a long, jagged scar in the steel plates. It was the welding scar where the freighter's beam had burned a leak in the hull.

He walked back into the main salon to find her seated before one of the portholes, staring out at the sprinkled constellations of the stars. He saw her cringe slightly as he stepped out of the corridor, but she didn't look up.

He moved over to the liquor cabinet, got out a fumbler, and poured himself a stiff three fingers.

She gave a soft, brittle laugh. "It's—it's quite a coincidence, isn't it?" she stammered shakily. "I was—I helped them on the forward gun battery. I'm the one who— who got you with that beam, Kim…"

Then she rose and stalked swiftly to her stateroom. The door clicked shut with grim finality.

Kim stood staring after her and sipping his drink, silently.

He was standing late watch in the control pit when he heard her moving around, below. Pots clattered in the galley.

When he came down, she had dinner prepared. They seated themselves and ate without speaking. Then she put down her fork, sighed timorously, and looked up.

"I apologize for acting silly, Mr. Rothman," she said coldly. "I have no right to be that way. I've accepted your services, no questions asked—I should have been aware of the circumstances."

Kim pushed his plate aside, hardly having touched his food, took out his cigarettes, and drew one alight. He studied his hands absently. "You're quite right, Fran," he acquiesced.

She gave an angry grimace and hot tears glittered in her eyes for an instant. "But—whatever could make you do such a thing?" she demanded with a suddenly shrill voice.

Kim raised his brows in feigned indifference, leaned back, and blew a faint cloud of smoke at the wall. "Fortunes of war, I suppose—"

"War? *What* war? It's the 'fortunes' you're after, isn't it? I suppose you'd kill for money—"

He faced her, then, his face without expression. "No," he said softly. "Not for money, Fran. For the lives, the freedom of others, perhaps—"

Fran buried her face in her hands.

"Lives? Freedom? Does that explain the attacks that have been made on so many space freighters going to Jupiter? The lives lost—"

"Those were corporation-owned freighters," Kim said coldly.

"Suppose they were?" She dropped her hands, glared at him accusingly. "Suppose the corporations of Earth do own and operate a few space freighters? The crews are better paid, get better medical care. Or is it the corporations?"

"It is," Kim nodded.

"But *why?* They don't enslave their employees. They aren't exploiting the Jovian Moons, fighting each other—the Earth government doesn't allow such ruthless measures, on Earth or anywhere else. They'd lose their colonial rights if they ever tried that. This—this isn't the Sixteenth Century."

"If that were all we were concerned with, there'd be no pirating," Kim retorted firmly. "As it is, we aren't just pirates—we're privateers, paid by the free settlers of Mars and Venus. They get the loot of our raids."

"Because you can out-bid Earth's prices?" she snapped hatefully. "That's how you make your 'fortunes,' isn't it?"

"Most of us are paid a flat fee per trip, Miss Freemont. We are not paid for the loot. We stop the freighters; crews from Mars or Venus board the freighters, capture them, and go home with them."

Fran stared at him, then shook her head. "I can't believe that, Kim," she said quietly. "That it's the free settlers of Mars or Venus who're really to blame? No, Kim—they could never get by without Earth—"

"No, they couldn't. But Earth has almost forced them to get by without her, charging them prices they can't pay."

Her eyes narrowed contemptuously. "Do you realize a space credit is evaluated at one thousand dollars in Earth currency?"

"It's materials and machinery that make values," Kim said caustically. "Not figures on paper. But I didn't say the free settlers were altogether to blame. We spacemen were the ones who turned pirate..."

"Robbing the rich to give to the poor, I suppose...?" she taunted.

"Attacking corporation-owned freighters because they spell the end for us." Kim replied. "The crews of those freighters work for the corporations, not themselves—they're even being trained by the corporations, rather than the Space Academy—"

"That's reason enough to kill them?"

"They're a bunch of white-collar workers who jump only when they get the word from the main office!" Kim shouted. "They've proved, many times, that you can't make decisions in which settlers' lives are at stake from any plush office on Earth. If they were worth the title of spacemen, they'd have seen that the Mars and Venus settlers got their supplies from

Earth whether they could pay for them or not!" He slammed his fist on the table and slumped back in his chair, scowling.

Fran sat perfectly still far a moment, then touched her napkin to her lips and rose. "I don't think there's any point in discussing this further," she said coolly. Then she walked to her stateroom. The door closed gently.

Kim smoked three cigarettes in rapid succession, then got up and steamed the dishes.

RELATIONS were rather strained, from then on. Fran kept mostly to her stateroom, coming out only to prepare meals.

Kim told himself that he didn't care. And he didn't—about some things. He ate little, picking at his food. His hair grew long, bushy. A week's stubble of tough, black beard sprouted from his cheeks. He virtually shunned the large shower-room in the crew's quarters. His mouth twisted into a habitual scowl. He slept fitfully.

She came unexpectedly into the salon, one day, and stopped, her face turning bone-white.

He was standing at the other end of the salon, stripped to the waist, rolling his shoulders, flexing his arms, and whipping his guns from his holsters in blurred practice draws.

She turned slowly and walked out.

For a long while after she was gone, Kim stood staring after her. Then he took a flask from the liquor cabinet, retired to his bunk in the crew's quarters, and drank himself to sleep.

When they began nearing the proximity of Earth, he set up the Schmidt lens scope in the control pit and began taking observations of the planet. It was a giant blue sphere on the lens, a bright crescent of light and a dim blur of darkness. There were the brown patches of boiling equatorial deserts in Africa, Australia, and North America, the verdant green vegetation near the Poles. He studied the Mississippi and Amazon Bays in the Western Hemisphere, that once were peaceful farm-valleys, and the channels and lakes and ten thousand islands in Central Russia. It was winter in the Northern Hemisphere, and there was a tiny patch of white in the Arctic Ocean, all that remained of the polar ice and the last great Ice Age, 14,000 years ago.

Earth had became quite a bit warmer since then.

Kim felt no affection for the planet. He had been to Earth only once, and then just to the great Sahara Spaceport. His interest was prompted solely by the fad that, like all planets, the Earth had a tendency to wobble about erratically on her orbit. A man coming in on a long trajectory could never be sure which side of the Equator he'd come down on.

But he left the Schmidt scope mounted in the control pit. And as he returned on his next watch, he found Fran peering into it. He wriggled past her and crawled down into his seat. Neither of them spoke. But Fran stayed.

The radio began to distinguish signals from star-noise soon after that. Kim spent long hours beside it with notepad and stylus, listening to messages and scribbling notations. It wasn't long before he knew there were six Space Fleet dreadnoughts swinging in orbit around the Moon, and their position and motion along that orbit. He plotted the trajectories of space-liners and freighters plying between Earth and the Moon, and leaving and approaching those two bodies from the other planets. With that information, he plotted his own approach along a trajectory that would touch no radar fields, one that would bring the *Voodoo* safely down to Earth without being detected.

He opened the chart locker and dug out the Earth maps at dinner. "Where's the Chao-Tang estate?" he asked.

She pointed it out on the map of Asia, a spot on the slopes of the Khangai Mountains, just north of the Gobi plains. "There are large cattle and sheep ranches on the Gobi," she explained practically. "Large vineyards in the Valley of the Kara Nor. People are widely scattered and most of them wouldn't know a spaceship if they saw one. There are deep hardwood forests on the slopes of the Khangai, and only a few country estates and isolated lumber camps. You can hide the *Voodoo* easily in that country."

Kim nodded absently. "I'm more concerned with getting down there unnoticed. A sweep across the Indian Ocean and through Central China would seem the best bet—more cattle industries in that jungle grass land—"

The Earth grew to a huge, swollen ball, steaming with dense atmosphere. It crept across the black emptiness of space and the *Voodoo,* like a tiny, invisible needle, hurtled toward it, vanished into it…

THE ravine was a deep, narrow gash in the hillside, with steep walls of ancient, crumbling rock. The *Voodoo* rested snugly in the bottom of it, with nothing to reveal her presence except a few blackened trees at the end of the ravine, seared by her force-screen as she slithered over them.

She had arrived at night. Now, it was morning. Fran's slim, lovely figure came scrambling up to the top of the ravine with breathless eagerness. She stood still, her hair blowing about her head and her scant garments molding against her body, staring out over the wide valley to a distant line of sheer bluffs. She laughed musically as Kim came stumbling up after her, straining muscles he seldom used.

Her face shone with radiant happiness as she skipped merrily ahead. The wind made a low, sweet sighing sound in the tall stands of hardwood timber that cloaked the surrounding hills. Leaves rustled and bushes whispered. Birds made weirdly beautiful sounds in the trees.

She stopped, laughing with sheer, bubbling joy, and looked back at Kim.

He stood at the top of the ravine, staring about with a strange puzzlement. This wasn't home, to him—it was a new, unknown planet. The blue dome of the sky seemed to shut him in; the puffy white clouds and the trees around him seemed fragile, somehow futile things. Only the worn, crumbling rock beneath his feet told him they were neither fragile nor futile. The beauty of the surroundings was strange to him; and being strange, seemed garishly ugly.

He stood darkly against the sky, a lost, lonely figure.

Fran turned and walked back to him.

"I know where I am, Kim," she said quietly. "It's only a few miles to a traffic lane. I can signal a ride from there on." She held out her hand, smiling wistfully. "I guess it's time for the lady and the pirate to—to say goodbye."

Kim gazed down at her, soberly. Then he grasped her small firm hand; shook it. She stood close to him for a moment, then gave a sad, little shake of her head, turned, and walked quickly off into the dark, frowning trees.

Kim watched her go, silently. Then a frown crossed his brows as he turned back to stare out over the valley.

There, miles away, on a neighboring slope where the timber stood thickly. He'd noticed it in the radarscope as they came down through the darkness, wondered if it were a natural formation.

Now he knew it wasn't. It was a mile-long streak through the dense trees, beginning with blackened tops and becoming black, naked trunks and finally a deep gash where the trees had been burned down to stumps.

Another spacecraft had landed on the slopes of the Khangai Mountains.

CHAPTER FOUR
The Eagles Gather!

THERE was a dry gully between the trees. The blackened fireburn ran into the gully.

There was a man sitting on a rock at the top of the gully, holding a Chavez beam-rifle across his knees.

Kim loosened his guns in their holsters and stepped out of the dense brush, facing the sentry.

"Don't lift that Chavez," he warned flatly.

The sentry started, gaped at him. Kim noted that the man wore the usual, nondescript shorts and jacket of a spaceman.

"My name's Rothman," he said. "Wind up that wrist-set you're wearing and tell your boss-man below I'm coming down for a talk."

"Huh?" the sentry grunted dumbly. "Oh! Yeah—sure." He raised his left arm, flipped a stud on the tiny transceiver set strapped to his forearm, and spoke into the grid. "Jehupat calling from topside."

"What is it, Jehupat?" a harsh, metallic voice spat back.

"Somebody named Rothman wants to see Black Dog."

"Wait a minute…"

Kim's right-hand gun was suddenly covering the startled sentry. "I don't just *want* to see him, bucko, I'm *going* to see him…"

Before the sentry could reply, the tiny radio spat again.

"It's okay, Jehupat. Let Rothman come down."

"Now, that's just fine," Kim murmured softly. He walked past the sentry, turned, and glanced down into the gully.

It was just deep enough to hold the fat, blackened hulk of the refitted space freighter. Kim knew instantly that it was a pirate craft. Freighters were slow and clumsy, but the gun-batteries bristling from their turrets along the bulging flanks could equal the firepower of any Space Fleet dreadnought.

He gave the tense, silent sentry a parting glance and started down the faint path that led to the freighter's airlock.

As he reached the bottom of the gully, he spotted the table and chairs that had been set up in the shadow of the steep clay bank, near the airlock. He studied the huge man seated behind the table, watching him.

The thick airlock portal stood open. The dark portholes along the ship's looming side revealed no glimpse of inner movement. The whole set-up stank, Kim thought. It was ominously silent.

The man at the table was a vision to behold. He had a segmentated flak helmet, looking like an oversized steel pineapple, on his head. He had thick, bushy black brows, a tremendous knob of a nose, and a great wealth of black beard. He was naked to the waist, built somewhat like an overgrown gorilla, and he wore scarlet shorts and shiny black boots. Moreover, there was a rich purple cloak thrown over one shoulder, and the cloak was decorated with a small, black human skull.

"Well!" the vision exclaimed, in a voice that boomed thunderously. "Mr. Kim Rothman, is it? Come sit down…"

"Everybody knows me," Kim quipped in wry disgust.

"Proper introductions. Of course, of course—forthcoming," the black beard boomed. "I am Captain Black Dog MacSneary."

"Captain of what?" Kim asked in sweet innocence. He was glad he had his gun out, seeing the big .055 mm. Maxim pistol on the table.

"Captain, sir, of the good ship *Satanis…*" MacSneary announced. To prove his point, he turned and spat fondly on the blackened hull. "A blasted space pirate like yourself, sir," he added with consummate pride. "The *only* space pirate who looks the part, damn me, and has *three* Second Officers to boot! They're covering you from the Number Three port turret, up there—a blonde, a brunette, and a redhead…"

"Well, goodness sakes," Kim taunted, grinning. "I can hardly wait for the elephants."

MacSneary's eyes squinted almost shut. "A bit more impertinence, Mr. Rothman, and you may even hear the calliope."

"Let's cut the routine short, Mac," Kim retorted. "What're you doing around here?"

MacSneary gave a snaggle-toothed smile. "I have a captive chained below decks, Mr. Rothman. Picked him up a few days after you cleared Ceresport and came here with him, passing you on the way, I believe, and arriving first." He leaned aback and tugged at his beard, chuckling. "The captive, sir, is Mr. Hiram Tucker, formerly First Officer of the freighter *Walrus*. Sound interesting?"

"Go on," Kim prompted.

"Mr. Hiram Tucker happens to be a third-generation native of the planet Venus," MacSneary obliged. "Twenty years ago, he was a close friend of a reptile hunter named Walter Tucker—no relation—who died, at that time, of fungus fever in Venusport. Intriguing?"

"Wouldn't be the reptile hunter who told of the froggish Venusians?" Kim asked thoughtfully.

MacSneary grinned. "You know perfectly well it was, Mr. Rothman. And I'm here to tell you you're not going to grab the sacred treasure of the Venusians if I can get at it first…"

"Treasure?" Kim's ears perked up.

"But of course. The treasure of deadly metal that no man could approach and live…" MacSneary spread his broad, powerful hands, conclusively. "The treasure old man Tucker babbled about before he died."

"Hmmm…" Kim hummed, scratching his chin with the muzzle coil of his gun. "There's a treasure, is there?"

"Undoubtedly. That scientific chap, Thompson, has returned and bore out Tucker's tale of the Venusians. Why, then, shouldn't the part about the treasure be true?"

Kim stared at the pompous, old pirate. Then he holstered his gun, walked forward, grabbed a chair, and straddled it. "Mac, old boy," he chided, "you didn't come here just to tell me all these sweet nothings. Want a cut in the deal?"

"On the contrary," MacSneary retorted, "I shall cut the whole pie, thank you. At the moment, my dear fellow, my henchmen are out picking a ripe plum named Miss Frances Freemont whom you so graciously dropped into our midst. When they return, I shall contact Miss Freemont's relatives and ask them for the exact location of this tribe of Venusians in exchange for the young lady. I believe Mr. Wu Chao-Tang, Director of the Biochemical Research Department, will be happy to cooperate."

Then he planted his big hands on the tabletop and leaned toward Kim. "My advice to you, sir," he said in a low, menacing grumble, "is to get out while you still have a whole skin."

Kim rose to his feet, slowly. "Will you stand up for it?" he asked. "Or do you want it sitting down?"

MacSneary flashed his snaggle-toothed grin. "I perceive, sir, that I must show you my hand. There…" He gestured toward the looming, black hull.

Kim glanced upward, then froze. A steel plate had swung open in the hull, and three young girls stood braced in the opening. They each held a Chavez rifle centered directly on his chest. There was a blonde, a brunette, and a redhead, all attractive, all wearing pistols belted around their thighs and not a stitch of anything else.

"Three aces, Mr. Rothman!" MacSneary chortled.

Kim shrugged. "I guess you win the pot."

"Thank you. Good day, Mr. Rothman. Have a pleasant journey…"

Kim turned and walked back up the faint, narrow path.

FRAN'S footsteps left a clear trail from the top of the ravine, where he'd left her. Kim followed in a dead run, branches and thorny brambles tearing at him mercilessly.

It was just possible that MacSneary had slipped up in arranging his timetable. Obviously, the old pirate had expected him to see the fire-burn, Kim concluded, and knew he would come to investigate. Thus, the men who were to kidnap Fran were watching the *Voodoo* when he and Fran emerged. Then they followed Fran until she was a safe distance away, beyond earshot. While they were doing that, Kim had moved swiftly—had spotted the fire-burn immediately, while MacSneary couldn't have expected him to do—had been early to reach the *Satanis*.

That left enough time for MacSneary's men to capture Fran; it didn't leave enough time for them to get halfway back with her.

Kim stumbled, careened against a rough tree trunk, and plunged onward. The trail wandered around the brow of a tall, frowning peak and zigzagged down a steep incline. He stumbled again, lost his footing on the loose shale, sprawled on his face and rolled.

He climbed to his feet, cursing, and went on more cautiously.

They were at the bottom of the incline, starting up. There were three of them, young, sturdy lads. They wore skimpy loin-strings supported by belted guns at their thighs. And one of them was wearing Fran Freemont, draped over his brawny shoulder. She was trussed up, gagged, and no trouble at all.

Kim proved to be another matter.

He stepped out of the trees above them with a gun in each hand. He wasn't a welcome sight, or a pleasant one. His wild beard and bristling hair were caked with dust, his garments were torn to shreds, and his body was creased with livid red welts and smeared with dirty sweat.

And the first thing he did was blow the legs out from under the young, sturdy lad carrying Fran, before she could be pulled down and used for a shield. The young lad fell into the boiling, blood-drenched dust and Fran fell on top of him. The young lad screamed in agony, a scream that tapered off into a moan of unconsciousness.

Kim spoke to the remaining two.

"Lay down on your bellies and stretch your arms over your heads, or you'll lay down the same way he did!"

They complied hastily.

He walked over, jerked the guns from their holsters, and hurled them off into the brush. Then he dragged Fran off the bleeding, legless body and deposited her in the cool shade of a tree. Her eyes were glazed with terror. He ripped the gag from her mouth and slapped her lightly on each cheek. He nodded in satisfaction as each cheek showed a spot of color, then returned to business.

"Pick up your colleague, gentlemen," he ordered to two prostrate men, "and carry him back to MacSneary with my compliments. Tell him he has exactly one hour to leave Earth."

Again, the results were swift. The two men, and half another, scrambled up the steep incline.

Kim untied Fran and began massaging her wrists and ankles, warming the circulation back into them. "We've got to get back to the *Voodoo,*" he said quietly. "Think you can make it?"

"I—don't know," she mumbled through stiff lips. "They—*kidnapped*—me!"

"We were followed from Ceres by a character named MacSneary," he explained briefly. "He'll no doubt stop at nothing to get his hands on you. Kidnapping's the only way he could get what he wants, with no trouble from the Space Fleet or the Earth police."

"What—what'll we do?"

"Get back to the *Voodoo.*"

"F—fight them?"

Kim shook his head and stood up.

"They out-gun us. C'mon."

"B—but what—" She gasped dizzily as he hauled her up to her feet.

"We'll radio the Space Fleet," he said grimly.

She took a stumbling step, then grabbed at him, staring up at him. "But—but that means you will—"

"No time for regrets, Fran. *Start walking...*"

IT took only a General Distress call to arouse the Space Fleet dreadnoughts out near the Moon. Kim gave them a terse description of the *Satanis* and her armaments, her position and probable intentions; he broke connections when the Space Fleet operative demanded identification. *That cooks my goose!* he thought grimly.

But Fran apparently had different ideas. She pushed him, retuned the ship's radio, and began calling into the mike. "Francis Freemont calling Chao-Tang. Francis Freemont to Chao-Tang. Can you hear me?"

And the radio speaker blared back, clearly. "Chao-Tang to Miss Freemont, we hear you most definitely. Decrease your modulation please."

Minutes later, a sleek, teardrop craft came skimming over the *Voodoo* on whistling rotar-blades.

"Come on," Fran prompted, tugging at Kim's arm. "You were willing to give up everything for me—and I'm not leaving you here for the Space Fleet."

He stumbled after her in a daze, was grasped by eager hands that pulled him into a cool, cushioned interior. He felt Fran's soft, warm body crowd in beside him, then the floor tilted and they were rising.

Shock and fatigue crept through him like a stealthy cloud of black unconsciousness. Just before it rolled up over his eyes, he caught a glimpse through a transparent roof of the clean, blue sky. Tiny specks were circling downward—swift, powerful little Fleet scout cruisers...

The eagles were gathering.

HE woke up between crisp, white sheets. Cool salve covered his welts and scratches. His cheeks were smooth, clean-shaven. His whole being felt listless. His nerves were dulled.

Had he passed out? *That* had never happened before.

The walls of the room were dark blue. The ceiling had thick, glossy beams of rich mahogany. The window was a large, arabesque opening on his right, looking out on green treetops and blue mountains in the distance. The door was a low, narrow slot...

A small, brown head poked in through the door, then withdrew before he could catch more than a glimpse of it. There was a soft laugh.

A moment later, a tall, slender Oriental came in. As he walked over to the bed, Kim realized that the bed was resting flat against the floor. The man had tilted eyes, tawny skin, and a white goatee. He was old, but husky, well muscled. There was a black skullcap on his baldhead and a blue silken robe fell to his ankles.

"I see you're among us again, Mr. Rothman," he said calmly. "Permit me to introduce myself; I am Yin Chao-Tang."

"Where's Fran?" Kim asked. He was surprised at his weak, grating voice.

"Miss Freemont is resting," Yin replied. "She would not leave your side until we had assured her thoroughly that you were beyond the crisis." There was a faint humor in his tones.

"Crisis?" Kim rasped.

"You have been ill." Smiling, Yin stepped over to a low seat and eased himself into it, cross-legged. "With all that exertion, you were weakened and fell victim to mountain fever, Mr. Rothman. It's a local virus infection."

Kim's eyes widened. "No—immunity!" he gasped.

Yin nodded. "Having spent your life in the controlled environment of spacecraft and domed cities, you had not developed immunity to such a disease. You were struck down rather swiftly. It was fortunate that we could give you treatment immediately, or it would have been fatal."

Kim laughed shakily. "Should have known—always clear through Medical before visiting a planet—"

"You should have medical examinations and inoculation against a new planet's diseases," Yin agreed. "Most people new to this region contract our mountain fever; it causes them to sneeze. But you were helpless against it. Immediate treatment saved you from a serious attack."

Kim stared at the ceiling. His breathing was shallow. Hunger gnawed at his stomach. "How long?" he rasped.

"Four days and five nights," Yin answered readily. "This is the morning of the fifth day. Miss Freemont did not sleep for four nights."

Another robed figure came through the door. A slender girl with coal black hair and blue eyes, wearing a scarlet robe that sheathed her in shimmering flame. She carried a bowl on a tray.

"Your broth has arrived," Yin announced, rising. "Eat, then rest, Mr. Rothman. We shall talk later."

THE next morning, Kim rose, bathed, and dressed himself in the silken blouse and slacks laid out for him. The slender girl led him out on a sunlit terrace and brought him a breakfast fit for three men. He polished it off, neatly.

He settled back contentedly over coffee and cigarettes. There was a comforting view of dark, timber-clad mountains and rolling, green slopes of vineyards and the silvery ribbon of a small stream. He had gradually grown accustomed to the scenery, had begun to feel appreciation for its strange, peaceful beauty.

He was in an excellent mood for what came next.

A slender figure materialized in the wide doorway opening out on the terrace.

"Kim!" Fran cried. Then she dashed out and threw her arms around him and clamped her lips on his.

Kim untangled himself somewhat dazedly. "—Um— uh—good morning," he said, placing his cigarette carefully on the ashtray. Then, somehow, he got tangled up again.

Fran laughingly struggled up out of his lap and stood staring down at him with bright, shining eyes. "My!" she exclaimed breathlessly. "You've certainly got your strength back."

"Strong constitution," Kim grinned devilishly. "Step back and do a slow turn, once, so I can see that—that thing you're wearing…"

"Would you *believe it?* Earth fashions changed in just the *short time* I was away."

She moved back with an impish grin, raised her arms, and did a slow pirouette before him. Kim whistled his admiration of her natural attributes, but her costume made him want to laugh. It was a bright green one-piece tunic, but it was transparent—she wore a black G-string under it, and there were little black dragons embroidered across the top.

Fran pouted at his derisive chuckle. "Well, it's what they're *wearing,*" she protested.

Kim looked vaguely puzzled. "What's *who's* wearing?"

"The—oh, you wouldn't understand—" She cast a soft smile at him. "I'm going to have breakfast," she announced with a pert toss of her head. "But you're going in to have a talk with Uncle Yin."

"Um?" He looked up, startled. "Did I do something?"

She frowned irritably. "You haven't—*done* anything, dear. It's just that Uncle Yin wants to *talk* to you."

"But I'd rather talk to you, first. I'll see him later."

"Kim—" She slumped into the chair across from him. "Don't be difficult," she pleaded. "Just do as I say—please. You'll find Uncle Yin in the study. Mei Ching will show you the way. Mei!" She clapped her hands, lightly.

The servant girl came gliding out the doorway.

"Show Mr. Rothman to the study," Fran commanded.

"Well, la-de-dah!" Kim exclaimed. He rose, kicking his chair back in irratiation. "Very well, your highness. I'll go settle old Uncle Yin's hash for you."

Fran looked somewhat shocked and even a little hurt as he strode away.

THE study was a long, low room in deep shadow. It had book-lined walls, narrow windows, and heavy teakwood furniture. Electric coals glowed bluishly in a small brazier, illuminating the tall figure with the white goatee who sat behind the massive table. Yin was garbed in a full-length black robe.

Kim stopped on the other side of the room when he saw his two Maxim guns, with belt and holsters, lying on the table before the old man. Then he approached, slowly. The guns were out of their holsters, their butts placed toward him.

This was it, then. The Chao-Tang family had taken him in and nursed him for Fran's sake. Now, it was a different matter. And he was a pirate.

Kim reached the table and picked up his guns, checking their gauges in the butt-plates. They were fully charged.

He slipped them into their holsters, then picked up the belt and buckled it about his hips. Old Yin Chao-Tang didn't move a muscle.

Kim faced him, squarely. "I want facts," he demanded. "What happened to Black Dog MacSneary?"

Yin raised a bony hand, protestingly. "It is as I suspected," he intoned. "You are accustomed to taking what you want."

"An oblique answer if lever heard one," Kim retorted. "I make my demands within reason, old man—the fellow who doesn't usually gets his head blown off. Now, what happened to MacSneary?"

Yin gave a sigh of resignation. "Very well, Mr. Rothman. But I must warn you that Miss Freemont will not be considered a reasonable demand. As for the pirate, MacSneary, I believe he anticipated your actions."

"Miss Freemont has a mind of her own, hasn't she?" Kim snapped angrily. "And I asked for facts, not your opinion."

"My apologies." Yin ducked his head in a bow. "Miss Freemont is free to make her own decisions, of course. But first, you must win her favor, Mr. Rothman. You will not find that easy. And if you try to take her by force, the family of Chao-Tang shall not rest until you are dead."

"So *that's* it," Kim said in a seething tone. "You crazy old fool, for that alone I ought to…"

Yin drew back in alarm. "Mr. Rothman. I must remind you that this is the house of Chao-Tang."

"That wouldn't make you less dead," Kim replied grimly. "But we'll skip that, for the present. Let's hear your facts..."

"Of course," Yin said stiffly. "We had best ignore the proprieties of the East. The pirate, MacSneary, gathered his crew into his spacecraft and shot straight up, smashing through the cover of the Space Fleet ships. The atmospheric resistance tore many pieces from his craft, including some gun-batteries. The Space Fleet caught up with it in space, but there were only a few persons left on it. The life boat had broken free with the others, and vanished."

"Uh huh," Kim grunted thoughtfully. "He knew I was calling in the Space Fleet, all right. But he wouldn't have bothered with Tucker—" Kim gazed down at Yin, sharply. "Was there a Hiram Tucker, First Officer of the *Walrus*, left on MacSneary's ship?"

Yin shook his head. "The Space Fleet reported no such captive."

Kim swore mirthfully. "Bluffing...that old devil..." He paced the room, chuckling to himself, then turned on his heel to face Yin. "What did you tell the Space Fleet?"

"Miss Freemont informed the Space Fleet commander that she had come here from Ceres in your deserter craft, the *Voodoo,* and that those other pirates had followed her," Yin answered glumly. "The Space Fleet commander assumed that someone with MacSneary owned the *Voodoo* and gave chase to recapture it. No mention was made of you."

"And the *Voodoo?*"

"It was confiscated by the Space Fleet, of course."

Kim scowled darkly. Loss of the *Voodoo* left him marooned here on Earth—a known criminal, a deserter.

"And now," Yin spoke with sudden vigor, "it is my turn to demand facts, Mr. Rothman. Why *did* the pirate, MacSneary, follow you and Miss Freemont to Earth?"

Kim stared at him, for a moment. That little matter had been completely forgotten.

Then Kim smiled, grimly. "Yin Chao-Tang," he said, in a soft, pleasant tone, "I'm glad you asked me that question."

CHAPTER FIVE
The Legend of Venus

"SO YOU can see where that leaves you, gentlemen," Kim concluded his explanation. "With this Hiram Tucker wagging his tongue all over Ceresport, that yarn about the Venusians' treasure will spread like wildfire. Every thief, pirate, murderer and adventurer in the Solar System will be racing with your expedition to find the Venusians, and fighting you every step of the way."

In the dark study with him was Yin, seated in a tall, straight-backed chair beside him. They faced a portion of the wall where a bookcase had been slid aside, revealing a giant television screen. On the screen in color, was a large desk and the back wall of an office, with a window opening on the slender towers of Manhattan Center, seat of the Earth government.

Wu Chao-Tang, Director of the Biochemical Research Department, was seated behind the desk. His image on the screen was vastly different from his brother, Yin, in appearance. Wu Chao-Tang was short of stature; his muscular torso was squat and powerful. He had a fuzz of white hair on the top of his head and was dressed in a modern jacket and slacks of blue plastisilk.

He smiled with a grim, tight-lipped humor. "I'm afraid you're right, Mr. Rothman," he said crisply. "It also occurs to me that you're a man who can best advise us as to how we must deal with these individuals you mentioned."

"There is only one way you can deal with them," Kim answered flatly. "You've got to strike first, before they do—and strike swiftly…"

Yin stirred irritably in his chair. "Learned brother," he addressed the screen, "I would hardly deem it advisable for us to accept the philosophies of—"

"Quiet, Yin!" Wu Chao-Tang snapped curly. "There is only one reason you are always left at home, my esteemed brother. It is where you belong."

He switched his gaze to Kim and smiled dourly. "Excuse the family squabbles, Mr. Rothman. Yin is always losing face. As for the expedition—" He paused, reflectively. "It's hardly a situation any group of scientists are endowed to cope with. I hesitate, now, to allow Miss Freemont to accompany them—"

"I think that's a wise decision," Kim observed, nodding.

"On the other hand," Wu continued, with a faint grin, "she is certified as a Second Officer. Suppose we signed you on as First Officer, Mr. Rothman?"

"The Space Fleet would pick me up as soon as they heard about it," Kim reminded him.

Wu chuckled mischievously. "In an emergency like this, I believe we could provide you with a set of false credentials—with another name, of course. What would you suggest?"

Kim considered for a moment.

"Make it Rogers," he decided. It was enough like his own name to be easily remembered.

Wu nodded. "Very well, Kim Rogers. A courier will arrive with the proper credentials for you within the next twelve hours. You and Miss Freemont will then report to me, here…"

It was Kim's turn to nod. "We'll do that," he agreed.

"Good. I'll see you then." Wu smiled, touched a button on the desk, and—the screen went blank.

Kim turned toward Yin, speculatively. "Tell Miss Freemont—" he began.

But Yin was gone. The chair was empty.

"I KNOW, Kim," Fran said later. "Uncle Yin told me."

She turned away as Kim approached her. Kim snorted in exasperation, whirled, and stamped out of her room. He roamed around the big house and out through the surrounding gardens, muttering to himself about "civilization" and spoiled females.

A courier in a natty blue uniform showed up that night, handed Kim a sealed packet, and departed. Kim opened the packet and examined the credentials of "Kim Rogers," finding them quite satisfactory. He even had a special Government Permit to go armed.

Dinner was served through a strained silence, with Kim, Fran, and Uncle Yin seated well apart at the long table and chewing through gloom-filled worlds of their own.

Afterward, Fran tapped his shoulder in the corridor. "Come on," she said. "We're leaving now."

She led him outside and through the moonlit gardens, walking briskly, and down the hill to a large hangar at the end of a long, hard-surfaced airstrip. A gang of mechanics was pushing a sleek jet plane out of the hangar.

Fran vanished up the entrance hatch and Kim crawled gingerly after her. He found her strapping herself into the seat behind the controls, wriggled into the adjoining seat in the small, pressurized cabin, and cast a doubtful frown through the plexiglass bubble at the plane's thin, swept-back wings and ram-jet pods.

"You sure this thing'll fly?" he asked.

"Buckle your seatstraps!" she replied tersely.

"Uh huh," he grunted. "You'd think these great Earth scientists would develop gravplates small enough for aircraft..."

Fran pressed her lips together tightly and slapped the starting switches. The plane trembled; she shoved open the throttles; and they hurtled forward with a swooshing roar.

Minutes later, Kim glumly conceded that the contraption would stay up. Fran handled the controls with a cool precision that won his grudging admiration.

"Got a cigarette?" she asked.

He dug them out, handed one to her, and puffed one alight himself. Lump mountains and green valleys speckled with tiny houses slid past below.

"You didn't do too well, Kim," Fran remarked. "I was rather disappointed in you."

Kim stared at her, blankly. "Uncle Yin?" he asked.

"Yes." She spoke in a calm, detached tone. "He's a favorite of mine."

"Uh huh," Kim sighed. "Guess I'm just a bull in the China shop."

"You almost sound proud of it."

"Could be I am." He scowled grimly. "What's so hot about Uncle Yin, anyway?"

"Why—he's so quaint, so Oriental..." she spoke protestingly. "I think he's a darling..."

Kim loosened his straps and twisted around so he was facing her. "Tell me something," he said. "Have you ever heard anyone say anything about Uncle Yin being his mother's favorite?"

Fran started visibly. "W—why, I think—yes. How did you know that?"

"It's a trait," Kim muttered. "Things like that are noticed quickly, out where I live."

"You mean he's a sissy?" Fran shook her head. "He's nothing of the kind, Kim. You don't know—"

"I didn't say he was, did I?" Kim cut her short.

"Then, what *do* you mean?" she demanded.

Kim puffed on his cigarette, breathed smoke through his nostrils, and turned away. "You wouldn't understand," he said.

She turned her head to look at him, then. "You'll never change, then, will you?" she murmured softly.

It was an irrelevant question; Kim ignored it.

THEY flew northward swiftly, swinging up over the Arctic Ocean. Other planes registered from time to time on their radarscope, and went flashing past, trailing a ribbon of white vapor. The sky grew dark and the stars twinkled out. Kim immediately began to feel more at home. Below, there were bright splashes of light where great industrial cities lifted their towering spires from the squat masses of atomic plants. Later, Fran looked down at the small, floating ice field.

"Did you ever notice that the blue-and-white symbol of the Earth government doesn't match the contours of Earth's continents?" she asked, musingly. "It's the old United Nations' symbol."

"It's fairly close, isn't it?" Kim responded.

She shook her head, smiling. "Just in general outline. It was designed before the polar ice melted, you see—that raised the sea level of the oceans."

Kim sighed indifferently and settled himself down to grab some sleep.

He awoke as they came skimming down onto a broad airfield. Tall towers loomed in the background, glowing softly in the early morning twilight. The plane's tires kissed the concrete and they rolled smoothly along the runway.

"New York Air Terminal," Fran explained. "A Department agent is waiting to escort us to our hotel. We're just in time for breakfast." She applied the wheel-brakes, deftly. The plane swung into a parking area.

A sleek, glass-topped car whisked them across a long causeway from the brown coastline of the Catskill cliffs to the man-made island of Manhattan Center. Entering the Center, they strolled along moving walkways on broad boulevards between the huge, pastel colored towers. Fountains tossed their spray in tropical gardens beneath stately palm trees.

There were few people on the streets at that early hour. Men hurried along, wearing the modern, loose jackets and slacks of bright plastisilk. Young women, like Fran, wore the thin tunics and G-strings. Elderly women were richly gowned.

Transparent roofs enclosed the streets; there was a faint, steady breeze from circulation fans. Subterranean traffic murmured beneath their feet.

Kim felt a sneaking tremor of fear, as though the flat, towering walls were closing in on him. It left him pale and miserable.

"I been sick," he quipped wryly.

Fran turned. "What?"

"Nothing."

They registered at a hotel and the uniformed, young agent who had guided them departed with a kindly grin. They had breakfast in a flowery, glass-enclosed nook, with soft music humming in the background. A robot trundled up to their table with a portable televiewer as they were having their last cup of coffee. It was Wu Chao-Tang; he wanted to see Kim Rogers at his office, immediately. Fran needed her beauty nap, she said apologetically.

Kim stalked out alone, swung aboard one of the moving walkways, and sneered at the mighty metropolis. He'd take

Level Nine any day! His walk was slowed to a few steps at a time as the walkways became crammed with people. His fear came back, for an instant. It was a greater mass of humanity than he had ever seen in his life—what must it be like in those industrial cities on the Arctic?

He looked at the individual towers, read the street-labels at the corners, and found his way to Wu Chao-Tang's office as easily as if he were charting his way around the Sun.

"You look unhappy, Mr.—ah—Rogers!" Wu exclaimed jovially, waving a hand that clutched a fat cigar toward the nearby chair.

"Guess I'm a savage," Kim replied, grinning. "Uncivilized." He sprawled into the proffered chair and took out a cigarette.

Wu smiled quietly. "History repeats itself, I suppose. Once, a cultured gentleman of the early American colonies wrote a letter to a friend, describing a visit paid to him by a backwoodsman of those times—are you familiar with history, Mr. Rogers?"

Kim's grin broadened. "If I remember it correctly, the gentleman asked the backwoodsman to be seated; and the backwoodsman complied seating himself cross-legged on the floor. The gentleman protested and finally persuaded the buckskin-clad huntsman to sit in a chair. The backwoodsman kept fidgeting, fearing the contraption would collapse under him."

Wu nodded. "You, sir, are a modern backwoodsman." He rose, paced around his large, streamlined desk, and approached the broad window looking out on Manhattan Center. "Three million people down there never heard of you, Kim," he added musingly.

Kim arched a querulous eyebrow. "Do I seem worried?"

"You wouldn't be; not you, Kim. There are five billion people on this Earth, living in their country homes and commuting by air to their jobs in the commercial centers. They have a high standard of living, thanks to atomic power—even though we haven't really harnessed it, yet. We've just converted its heat to steam, to kinetic power, to electricity. We still use plutonium processed from uranium."

Kim shifted uneasily. "What are you driving at?" he asked in a guarded, wary tone.

Wu swung around, chuckling. "There are only a half-billion souls out on the other planets, Kim. We five billions want the uranium of those worlds; your half-billion wants machinery, supplies. We charge high for it."

"Too high," Kim said curtly.

Wu walked back to his desk. "Yes," he agreed. "Too high. I can sympathize with that, Kim. But I'm only one of a few who know the conditions out there—one of a few, mind you, in five billions."

"So five billion people could be wrong..."

"True, unfortunately." Wu nodded. "And so, you are a pirate..."

"True," Kim mimicked mirthfully. "Unfortunately." He blew a perfect smoke-ring and peered across the desk at the stocky Oriental. "Which leads up to what?"

"The people of Venus," Wu said gently.

Kim's eyebrow went up, again.

"The *people* of Venus," Wu repeated with emphasis. "The natives, the Venusians, the natural inhabitants of that planet. If there are Venusians, Kim, why not Martians? How do we know? Neither of those planets has been even half-explored, yet."

"So?" Kim prompted.

"So the latest reports from Venusport tell of rumors that the free settlers are planning a revolution, there," Wu replied gravely. "A revolution, Kim, to win the planet for themselves—the planet that doesn't even belong to them.

And our own experts, here, are talking of the necessity of Earthmen migrating to those planets, to keep Earth from becoming overpopulated. Three million of us are healthy centenarians, Kim."

Kim pursed his lips, musingly. "Looks like a rough time for the Venusians."

"And for us," Wu amended softly. "The Venusians have atomic power, too…"

"Huh?" Kim jerked erect.

"Their 'sacred treasure' is a metal that glows with death," Wu said. "Anyone who approaches it is killed. None of the radioisotopes known to us can do that, Kim. We've always believed anything pouring out that much hard radiation would also release such intense heat that a man would be burned to a husk before any radioactivity could kill him."

Kim rubbed his chin, speculatively. "You're a biochemist, Mr. Chao-Tang—"

"And a geologist. The two fields are related in interplanetary studies."

"Have you asked a nuclear physicist about this Venusian treasure?"

Wu nodded. "Our most eminent physicists doubt if it exists at all. But Walter Tucker and DuBois Thompson said it did. They both died."

"Thompson—your investigator—died? I thought he was missing for twenty years—"

"And reappeared at Venusport two months ago, almost dead with fungus fever. He left a hand-written report. The medical examination revealed that his tongue had been cut out fifteen or twenty years ago."

"And this hand-written report?"

"Corroborated Tucker's earlier account in almost all details—the valley in the clouds, the temple, the village—"

"Who cut his tongue out?"

"Thompson called them 'the Toad men'…"

"And gave their location?"

"Yes. That's where our expedition is going." He went back behind his desk and sat down. "We may find nothing. It may be that there are no Venusians, that Thompson wandered half-crazed in the wilds of Venus for twenty years. But we've got to make sure."

"And if there are Venusians?"

"Then there are quite likely Martians," Wu replied. "And our invasion of their planets will result in colonial and, quite probably, interplanetary wars which could erase all life from the Solar System…"

CHAPTER SIX
The Cruise of the Eohippus

THE signal-gong chiming for Change-of-Watch stirred Kim out of a deep, fitful slumber He rolled out of his bunk, showered and dressed. His face was hollow-eyed and grim in the lavatory mirror as he trimmed his short, bristling beard.

Their three-weeks' cruise to Venus was becoming, in his considered opinion, a cruise of pure hell.

It had begun as soon as he stepped aboard the *Eohippus* as her First Officer. Wu Chao-Tang had come along to introduce him to Dr. Grogor Dimitrios, eminent biochemist-archaeologist, who was to be in charge of the expedition on Venus.

Dimitrios was a tall, handsome man with a beautifully muscled body—he wore skin-tight plastisilk coveralls that displayed his torso to best advantage. His coal-black hair was slicked back and his cold, dark eyes viewed Kim with contempt. Kim had known immediately that he'd made a mistake.

Earlier, he had told Wu, "I think the members of the expedition ought to be told my real identity and why I'm going along on the trip. MacSneary's still alive, and is bound to head straight for Venusport. He'll see that the Space Fleet officials there know about me as soon as I arrive, and the expedition members will learn about it anyway."

"And what will you do about the Space Fleet officials?" Wu asked.

Kim shook his head, grinning. "They won't bother me in Venusport. The free settlers would mob 'em if they bothered a space pirate."

So Dimitrios knew who he was, when Wu introduced them aboard the *Eohippus*. Dimitrios was a cold, logical scientist. He came straight to the point. "First," he said, "all weapons shall be locked in the ship's armory except the Maxim pistol that I shall carry. Second, Mr. Rothman or Rogers, you may be First Officer aboard this ship, but you had best remember that I am in complete charge of this expedition and what dealings it may have with the Venusians. Is that understood?"

Kim eyed him, gravely. "First," he replied in a soft, subtle tone, "I'd kill a few people before I ever surrendered my guns, and you're a fool to think otherwise—"

"Mr. Chao-Tang!" Dimitrios protested, turning to Wu.

"Dig your own grave," Wu told him, smiling.

"Second," Kim went on, firmly," I fully concede that you are in charge of this expedition. You're a scientist, Dr. Dimitrios, and you should have better knowledge of how to deal with any intelligent alien beings, such as the Venusians."

Dimitrios was flustered. "Why—uh—I hadn't thought you'd see that, Rogers. Perhaps I've underestimated you." His tone of surprised apology belied the hard anger that flared in his eyes. Dimitrios didn't like being made to appear ridiculous by a space pirate.

"And we'll forget about my guns," Kim told him, flatly.

"Of course." The scientist turned on his heel and walked off.

That had been the first incident.

Examining the ship's log, Kim learned vaguely that an Eohippus was either a South American beetle or a dawn-age horse or a species of Venusian fungus-tree; the geologists hadn't agreed which it was. He also learned that the good ship *Eohippus* was very weak in the power department.

She was a flat-bottomed, ugly-looking craft with rocket jets sprouting all over her nose, belly, and tail; she had a powerful radar and a souped-up force-screen, all of which was necessary for a ship that went plunging into the dense cloud-blanket over an unknown sector of Venus. Her grav-plates were also up to par. But for all this extra junk, she had only three hundred-thousand-horsepower atomic turbines.

Kim raised hell with the Spaceport Maintenance director until he got two extra turbines. Then Dimitrios tried to stop him from installing the turbines—that space was needed for extra equipment and instruments. Dimitrios threatened to call the Spaceport Guards.

Kim replied levelly that any Guards Dimitrios called would be killed, and the expedition would never leave Earth. Then he installed the turbines.

That not only made him less popular with Dimitrios, but prejudiced the rest of the expedition's members against him.

Fran remained friendly, if aloof; Kim was grateful for that. But it had hardly lasted through the first week of the trip.

Kim gulped down a scalding cup of coffee in the ship's galley and kicked his way up through the free-fall tube to the control bridge. It had been tough on Fran, he admitted, to remain friendly toward him, talking with him as they snared the Mid-Watch, dining with him in the ship's salon, chattering away with bright, feminine enthusiasm as they crawled through the ship's working innards on routine inspections. It had been tough because the others maintained a sullen silence in Kim's presence, shunned him whenever they could, gathered themselves around Dimitrios' imposing figure down on the passenger deck.

And Dimitrios had the figure to arouse any woman's interest. Also, he was a gentleman of culture and good tastes, with an exciting career both as an explorer and a scientist. On Earth, he was famous.

Gradually, Fran had become more and more civil toward Kim. She had begun to notice that the others were including her in their social boycott. For a woman, that was painful.

For Kim, it had been mildly satisfying.

HE swung lithely out of the tube and planted his feet on the grav-plated deck of the dark, silent bridge. Veils of glittering stars hung in the blackness above the transparent blister, flooding a milky glow down through it to etch the bridge in dim light and stygian shadow. Up forward, the silhouette of Fran's head and shoulders was outlined sharply against the ruddy glare of signal-lights on the control bank. Kim strolled toward her, glancing casually to either side where auxiliary instrument panels registered the functioning of the ship's mechanisms. Everything seemed shipshape— that, at least, hadn't troubled him, so far...

Fran glanced around as his light tread sounded on the deckplates behind her. The glare from the control bank illuminated her smooth cheek and slender throat, struck greenish highlights in her auburn hair. Kim felt a trembling urge to touch that soft hair, to kiss the smooth column of her throat—he stopped, clenched his fists tightly.

She stared back at him, a tall figure in rumpled jacket and slacks, standing in the starlight. "You're two minutes early," she announced coldly.

Kim shrugged and moved up behind her. "I'll take over, anyway. All readings check?"

"Check as computed," she answered. "There's a twentieth-place drift off course, but we can correct for that on our approach curve. Velocity increase is according to computed Solar drag. All circuits are clear." She rose gracefully from the acceleration chair, her slender slim body outlined revealingly through her thin tunic. "Shall I return for the Mid-Watch, or will you take it?"

"I'll take it, I guess," Kim said wearily, moving over to his own chair between the computer console and grid-table. "You needn't bother."

"Thanks." Fran bit the word out. "I'd rather listen to one of Dr. Dimitrios' discussions down on the passenger deck, anyway."

Kim sprawled into his chair, smiling grimly. "They're quite educational, I hear."

"Very." Fran grabbed up her pocketbook and belted it around her slim waist with quick, hurried movements. "I've—I've been thinking, too, Kim—" she stammered with a sudden breathlessness. "I think we should ask Dr. Dimitrios to pick up another team of officers at Venusport. I don't want to be Second Officer on the return trip. The way things are, we—we can't work together, Kim…"

"I hadn't intended to make the return trip, myself, anyway," Kim retorted in rising anger. "I'd be a fool to go back to Earth."

Fran stood frozen, staring at him, for a moment. "Oh…" she exclaimed softly. "I see. Of course, you saw no reason to mention that—"

"No need to." Kim looked up at her, critically. "Wu Chao-Tang knew it without being told," he added.

A strange, twisted little smile touched Fran's face in the starlight. She fumbled in her pocketbook, then held a folded sheet of notepaper out to him. "I was going to mention it," she said. "We received a message from Earth, a couple of hours ago. I think you'll be interested."

Kim's brows raised as he reached out and accepted the note. Fran swung on her tiny, spiked heel and strode back to the free-fall tube. Kim paused, watching her swing her trim figure into the tube, then flipped on the grid-table light and unfolded the small square of paper. The message was neatly inscribed in the space-frequency-receiver's small, compact type:

Wu Chao-Tang, Director of Biochemical Research Dept. Space Comm-station, Lunaport; Sahara Spaceport, Earth. Kim Rogers, First Officer *Eohippus*, en route Venus, 43099.6-D

To Rogers: Brother Yin Chao-Tang disappeared from Kanghai home shortly after you left there. Have just learned that Yin purchased scout cruiser *Voodoo* from government salvage with family funds, loaded provisions aboard, and blasted off for Venus. Suspect foolish brother wants sacred treasure of Venusians to save Oriental face. Do not trust him. If you see him, give him this message: if I ever see him again, I shall make him suffer for this dishonorable conduct.

Respectfully, Wu Chao-Tang; Manhattan Center, Earth, NW.

Kim refolded the message, slowly, and slipped it into his belt. He realized bitterly that Fran was blaming him for Yin's actions...

The radarscopes came to life with a clamoring of alarm-gongs, just three hours later. Kim threw the Nuclear Journal he'd been reading aside and whirled to the glowering scopes.

The next instant, the ship's radio buzzed raspingly with a General Distress call.

THE alarm-gongs brought Fran, Dr. Dimitrios, and the other members of the expedition—fourteen men and nine women, some of them sleepy-eyed and half-dressed, crowding onto the bridge. All of them exhibited a morbid fright induced by the uneasiness that had been growing among them.

Kim knew they instinctively distrusted him; he didn't exactly trust most of them, either. He didn't bother to look up as they came crowding around him, ignored them completely as he leaned toward the ship's radio panel, tuning its knobs and dials and chanting monotonously into the microphone: "Rogers of the *Eohippus* calling distressed lifeboat. Can you hear me? Rogers of the *Eohippus* calling distressed lifeboat—"

Dimitrios shoved forward through the babbling crowd and grabbed Kim's shoulder. "What is it, man?" he demanded. "What is it?"

Kim shrugged off his grasp and stared up at him. "A lifeboat swung in to intercept us on a collision orbit," Kim's voice was dry, emotionless. "They gave a General Distress call and cut off. I can't raise them."

"You mean they're adrift?" Fran cried anxiously. "Decelerate, then. We've got to pick them up!"

"I can't raise them," Kim repeated. "They won't answer."

"Probably they *can't* answer…" she retorted shrilly. "Their power probably ran out. They must be victims of a pirate attack—I know what that's like, Kim! *If you don't stop this ship, I—*"

She was already moving toward her chair, up forward, when Kim's dry tones stopped her. "The controls are already set to decelerate," he said, turning back to the radio. "We'll coordinate with them in twenty-seven minutes. I want you to remain here on the bridge and stand by while I board them." He looked up at Dimitrios, again. "Better unlock the ship's armory and issue weapons…"

"Why should I?" the tall scientist snapped. "A helpless lifeboat; the victims of an attack by one of your pirate friends aren't likely to attack us. And the pirate ship isn't around or it would show on the radarscopes—"

"Very logical," Kim snapped back. "A lifeboat drifting 'helpless' in millions of cubic miles of space, and yet they don't radio a General Distress call until we 'just happen' to almost ram into them. Would you like to bet these 'victims' aren't interested in the location coordinates of that Venusian village, which are tucked in our chart locker?"

Dimitrios straightened up, haughtily. "Very well, Mr. Rogers. I concede that there is a possibility of danger. Weapons shall be issued…"

"Thank you. Fran, stand by to check coordination vector." Kim turned to his computer panel, seeming to lose all awareness of anyone else on the bridge. Dimitrios led the others slowly back to the tube.

Minutes later, Kim passed them on the way down to the airlock room. Dimitrios was holding a Chavez rifle and instructing the others on its use. Kim snorted in disgust (in the whole expedition, only half the members had ever been in space; and then, few of them had been farther out than the Moon!) and continued on aft, pulled his spacesuit gear from its wall locker, and struggled into it.

Dimitrios came into the airlock room with his long, swinging stride just as Kim finished testing his suit's pressure and circulation system. "You're going out to the lifeboat?" the scientist asked.

"We can't allow them to board us without checking," Kim replied, fastening his guns back around his waist.

"I'll go with you," Dimitrios stated decisively, opening the locker that held his own spacesuit.

"I'd better handle this, myself," Kim said. "If they get me, it'll be up to you to protect the ship."

Dimitrios stopped, then turned around and stuck out his hand. "I've been wrong about you, Kim. You're all right." He was smiling quietly, a new respect in his eyes. He had no illusions about the dangers Kim might be going out to face— and, for the sake of the others, Kim was electing to go it alone…

Kim shook hands, firmly. "I'll contact you by radio if everything's all right," he said. Then he clamped down his fishbowl helmet and turned to the airlock. Pirate or not, he knew he had won Dimitrios' undying admiration. He shut himself into the airlock and switched on the air pumps, feeling pleased with himself, if a little impatient. The more civilized people were, it seemed, the longer it took them to learn…

He adjusted the rocket V-frame on his back as the outer portal swung open, then crawled out into the star-sprinkled darkness. He hooked his magnetic boot-soles to the hull and stomped up over the back of the ship into the full, blazing glare of the Sun before he spotted the lifeboat, a silvery streak of metal several thousand yards away. Abruptly he kicked himself away from the ship and glided out across the black emptiness, rockets flaming at the tips of his V-frame. It seemed so long ago since he had seen others do this—

HE crawled through the lifeboat's airlock and stepped down into the turbine room, gun ready. The ceiling lights glowed dimly on the dark, polished bulkheads and deck. Kim peered down at the deck, wonderingly. There were little brown spots of dried blood weaving along the deck-plates to the airlock.

There was a tense, heavy silence within the little ship.

He moved forward, cautiously, through the doorway into the shadowy bunkroom. His boots clicked loudly on the deck-plates, following the trail of the little brown spots.

A faint whimpering sound came from the side of the room. Kim whirled, then strode deliberately around a row of tall double-bunks and halted, his gun hanging loosely from his fist.

The woman was strapped into one of the bunks, her long, brown hair falling straight and stringy to the deck. He stared at her pinched, hollow-cheeked face, the thin, knobby arms and legs, the skin stretched taut over the rib cage of her starved body. Madness glowed in her sunken eyes. If Kim had ever seen her before, he couldn't recognize her now.

He turned and moved slowly, grimly, up toward the control room.

There was a brown pool of dried, peeling blood in the back of the control room, with two tiny burns of Maxim beams in the bulkhead above it. The Maxim pistol lay on the top of the grid-table, in the center of the room. And beyond the grid-table, sprawled in a seat at the side of the forward control bank, was the huge, muscular, fat-bellied figure of…

Captain Black Dog MacSneary.

His black beard was crusted with dried blood, but it was not his own. He stared up at Kim with a bright, dawning recognition.

"Rothman!" he exclaimed. "Damn me, I should've known! That message to 'Kim Rogers'—"

"Sit still!" Kim commanded harshly. He walked up to the grid-table, picked up the Maxim, and glanced at the gauge in its butt-plate. The charge was empty. He tossed it into the back of the room. Its sharp clatter against metal made an ear piercing crash in his helmet phones. Wincing, he unsnapped the helmet and rocked it back on his air tanks.

MacSneary rubbed grimy hands over his naked belly and laughed softly. "With the little beard you've grown, I hardly recognized you. So Rothman, the space pirate, has gone on the side o' Earth—"

"Stop acting, Mac," Kim snapped. "You laid to out here in this lifeboat after escaping the Space Fleet, didn't you? You planned to catch us on our Earth-Venus trajectory and have us pick you up on a General Distress call—"

"It was a bit of a gamble," the old pirate admitted, proudly. "We were a mite short o' rations, and it seemed for awhile you blasted fools never would show up—" He stared at the dried blood on the floor and chuckled softly.

Kim's eyes narrowed with growing horror. It was like a steel spring tightening up inside him. "The brunette—I found her," he murmured. "But the blonde and the redhead—you wouldn't have left *them* behind—"

His finger tightened on the trigger.

"Blonde?" MacSneary echoed in wide-eyed innocence. "Redhead? Delightful subjects, Mr. Rothman, but whatever *could* you be talking about?" Then he grinned and belched gently.

The complete, brazen frankness of the man left Kim sick with revulsion. He jammed his gun into his holster and swung away from the fat, grinning old pirate.

"Come on," he ordered flatly. "Do every single thing I tell you to do, MacSneary, or I'll start by blowing your arms and legs off—and the rest of you, inch by inch—"

He strode back into the bunkroom, stopped, and turned to face the doorway, MacSneary followed him, obediently. Kim pointed toward the bunk at the side. "Unstrap her," he ordered. "Pick her up…"

Flashing his snaggle-toothed grin, MacSneary waddled over to the bunk. He leaned over the girl, began working at the straps, and giggled softly.

The girl stretched her mouth open and screamed. She screamed and screamed...

THE lifeboat was left drifting in space as the *Eohippus* resumed its journey. Fran double-checked her instrument readings and nodded. "Course registers as computed."

Kim slid the covering back over his grid-table and settled back in his chair. "That's that," he said dryly.

Fran turned, looked at him, then got up out of her chair and walked over to him. She didn't say anything...She just climbed onto his lap, put her arms around him, and buried her face in the hollow of his chest.

Kim held her close and ran his fingers slowly through her long, silken hair. There didn't seem to be much he could say, either.

Footsteps sounded on the bridge behind them. Kim turned his head to look up into the pale, drawn features of Dr. Gregor Dimitrios.

"The woman's in sick bay," Dimitrios said huskily. "Starvation and shock, mostly—I think she'll pull through. The man—" He spoke the word with utter loathing. "We locked him in one of the staterooms."

"Thanks," Kim said.

Dimitrios wiped the sweat from his face with his palms, tried to wipe away the screaming and babbling of the woman as they had pulled the spacesuit off her...

He would never forget that, Kim knew. None of them would. Kim only felt dull and lifeless inside. He had seen it before.

"Keep a guard posted outside the stateroom at all times," he said. "MacSneary will do anything he can to get at our chart locker and learn the location of those Venusians."

"We'll—we'll have to take him to Venus—" Dimitrios stammered.

"And turn him loose in Venusport," Kim affirmed. "But we'll pass the word around. I wouldn't want to be in MacSneary's boots, then."

Dimitrios turned and stumbled back to the tube.

They've learned, Kim thought grimly; *they know what it can be like, now.*

Fran reached up and touched his smooth cheek. "You've shaved," she murmured. "Your beard's gone."

They were alone, in the faint starlight of the bridge. Kim made love to her, caressed her soft body, wanting her. But he suddenly realized that he wanted even more to make her happy; he thought of the peaceful, quiet little country homes on Earth—the Earth where he could never live...

He could never give her that. The disappointment was like a sharp knife twisting in his chest.

"Fran," he whispered. "I want to give you a home—"

She grew still in his arms, listening to his thoughts, almost. Understanding him—fully and completely, for the first time—

And wanting him to speak, to tell her all the little things, the fine things, the big, grand things that went through his mind. But Kim couldn't speak. And, calmly, she understood that, too.

"We'll make a home, Kim," she whispered. "Wherever we are—"

THE *Eohippus* was three days out from Venusport when Kim called a conference in his stateroom. It was a private conference with Dimitrios, alone. They mixed drinks and lighted cigarettes, sitting across from each other at the small reading table, and Kim opened the discussion with a statement that brought the scientist bolt upright.

"I've just been in radio contact with Venusport," he said. "The free settlers are in revolt..."

"Great Scott!" Dimitrios gasped. "They're fighting?"

"The Venusport operator said it was small-arms," Kim replied. "The colonial government has barricaded the domed city under multiple force-screens. The revolutionists haven't any gun-batteries, and Space Fleet troopers have kept them away from the ships at the spaceport field, so far."

"How—how did it start?" Dimitrios stammered, aghast.

Kim shrugged. "Some fool on Earth sent several shipments of machinery and supplies to Venusport at prices the settlers couldn't pay. The stuff was sitting out on the spaceport field, rusting. Government property, you see—the officials at Venusport couldn't do anything with it without Earth's authorization, the Space Fleet has to protect it, and now there's hell to pay."

"Can we get in at the spaceport field?"

"Probably. If the revolutionists have captured it by the time we get there, we can hold them off with our force-screen. They probably won't molest us after they've learned who we are."

Dimitrios gulped his drink down, turned to the liquor dispenser, and refilled his glass. "Man!" he exclaimed. "And I thought I had something to tell you…"

Kim glanced up, sharply. "What?"

"The pirate girl," Dimitrios explained, turning back to the table. "She's been up and around the past several days. Just a few hours ago, she slipped past our guard and went into that stateroom where we have MacSneary."

Kim arched an eyebrow. "Is he dead?" he asked casually.

The scientist gave him an incredulous glance, then took another fierce swallow of liquor. "Dead? No!" he exclaimed harshly. "You—you can hear them laughing, playing in there—"

They stared at each other, silently. Then Kim gave a slow shake of his head. "Sometimes," he muttered, "a woman can be more ruthless than a man."

"We called her to come out," Dimitrios blurted thickly. "She told us—"

"Leave her in there," Kim said. "It'll keep them out of our hair. If MacSneary was planning to do anything before we reached Venus, I think he'd have acted by now." He smiled grimly, adding, "Just see that they get their meals."

He sipped his drink, thoughtfully. Dimitrios was silent, brooding. Kim straightened, yawned, and dismissed his morbid thoughts with a dry chuckle. "You've got the expedition all planned out, I hope?"

Dimitrios nodded. "We'll pick up guides and mud-cats in Venusport—I hope. If this revolutionary uprising doesn't hinder us too much—"

"Best to get that done as quickly as possible," Kim advised curtly. "The sooner we get away from the zone of trouble, the less chance we'll have of getting mixed up in it." He paused, scowling. "There's a little business I want to look into, myself," he announced tersely. "I want to see if the *Voodoo* has arrived there, yet—"

"You expect trouble from Yin Chao-Tang?"

"I expect to find something," Kim admitted vaguely. "I'll tell you more about it when I've found it."

CHAPTER SEVEN
The Venusian Revolt

IT was an acknowledged fact among all spacemen that Venus was the hardest planet in the System on which to make a landing. First, like all planets, Venus wobbled so that no blind instrument landing could be computed. Second, Venus was hidden beneath her dense cloud blanket, so that no direct observations could be made of her surface. Third, her surface was a nightmare of low swamplands and tremendous mountain ranges that towered miles into the clouds. Fourth, radar patterns were too vague at over ten thousand miles, so that no radar observations could be made until a ship was actually making its approach.

Every ship that approached Venus had to hover above the clouds, make radar observations, check their maps, and travel around the planet to the Keyhole Gap in the Misty Mountains, a deep cut in the giant peaks that gave them room enough to maneuver down to a landing on the spongy field at Venusport. As yet, Venusport was the only known landing site on the planet.

Such maneuvering demanded close teamwork. Kim watched the radarscopes, plotted their course down from second to second, making split-second changes when necessary. Fran controlled the massive spacecraft, keeping it poised delicately on its grav-plates in the merciless gravity pull of Venus, guiding it with deft touches on the firing-keys.

The *Eohippus* came floating down out of the swirling mists, a black, six hundred-foot blob of fat hull blurring out of rolling clouds burned orange-red and shot with gold from the penetrating infra-red rays of the hidden Sun. Port and starboard rockets whispered their throaty murmurs as the huge ship bellied down to the soft mud of the immense spaceport field. Her hull squished ponderously into the mud as the grav-plates faded off.

And Kim collapsed back into his chair with an explosive sigh of relief. He just barely saw, through his fatigue-dimmed eyes, Fran's pale, tense features as she turned to smile back at him. Her cheeks glistened with sweat.

Kim took out his cigarettes, ejected one for himself, and tossed the pack to her. They both needed a smoke.

Feet banged up the ladder-rungs and Dimitrios heaved himself up out of the tube. "Well done!" he exclaimed jovially. "That was surely the neatest Venus landing that I've ever seen—congratulations!"

"Nothing to it," Fran muttered sourly, pushing a damp strand of hair back from her forehead.

"Stop jumping around," Kim reprimanded him, gruffly. "We've settled down far enough in this muddy goo, already."

Dimitrios chuckled, perching himself on the edge of the grid-table before Kim. "You've called Venusport Medical to come out?" he asked affably.

"I have not," Kim retorted. "I'm not going to lift my little finger for a single, blasted thing until the goose bumps fade off of my goose-bumps. We gently grazed a twenty-mile-high cliff back there, and the whole shebang came down in an avalanche…"

"Better get Spaceport Repair out here, too, when we call in," Fran commented with the practical mysticism of a woman.

Dimitrios jerked around, stared at her in open-mouthed shock. "I didn't feel—I didn't hear anything," he stammered. "Were we struck by something? What's the damage? Why didn't our screen—"

Kim, whose mind had grown somewhat accustomed to Fran's feminine thought-patterns, interpreted: "We need Spaceport Repair to take a look at our air-purification unit."

"Oh…" Dimitrios seemed somewhat flustered. "Isn't it working?"

"Been kicking up a fuss ever since we left Earth," Fran spoke glumly around her cigarette. "You can't expect top efficiency when you buy a used ship, though," she added, stretching luxuriously. "This old crate has seen better days."

"I suppose so," Dr. Gregor Dimitrios muttered. Then, he seemed to regain his composure. "Look here," he said. "I want to get Medical out here and get past Quarantine as quickly as possible. I've got to get into the Governor's Tower in Venusport and file authorization for our expedition and line up mud-cats and cat-drivers."

"Keep your shorts on." Kim said. "First, take a good look out there at the field…"

Dimitrios and Fran both peered out through the bridge's transparent blister. They saw a vast, sprawling, muddy field littered with the blackened hulks of spacecraft; while off in the distance, the dim blur of the giant dome of Venusport rose vaguely into the sifting orange-red mists.

Then they both realized what he meant. At either end of the field were huge torpedo-shaped hulls bristling with gun turrets: Space Fleet dreadnoughts. And at the far end of the field, opposite the dim Venusport dome, there were brilliant, little flashes of light. Wicked sputtering little flashes. The kind made by Maxim pistols and Chavez rifles. The spaceport field was under small-arms siege.

"We can probably get into Venusport through the underground cargo tunnels," Kim mused thoughtfully. "But it looks like you may have to get more than *official* authorization, Dimitrios, if we're to drive an expeditionary convoy of mud-cats out through the ranks of those rebel forces…"

"Hmmm… 'Fraid you're right," Dimitrios admitted. "This blasted revolt may hold us up."

"Maybe it won't," Kim refuted mildly. "I want you to go into Venusport alone, Dimitrios. Have a chat with the officials about this revolt and about our expedition. And find out whether they know I'm Kim Rothman, space pirate—if Yin Chao Tang has arrived safely, they probably did."

Dimitrios frowned his disapproval. "Well—if it worries you—"

Kim gave a snort of disdain. "All the free-booters and outlaws of Venusport are probably out there helping those rebels fight!" he pointed out, impatiently. "If Yin Chao-Tang's been spreading word around Venusport that I'm a pirate after the Venusian treasure, those rebels are going to know about me and like me. Maybe I could make a deal with them to get our mud-cat convoy through."

"Oh…" Again, Dimitrios was flustered. "I—ah—I see," he said. "Then you and Miss Freemont will remain aboard ship until—"

"Fran will remain aboard ship," Kim corrected, "ready to clamp down our force-screen in case those rebels break through the Space Fleet lines. You will go in to pow-wow with the chiefs. I've got some personal business to attend to." He blew smoke through his nostrils, grinning devilishly, then leaned forward and flipped on the ship's radio. "Now, I'll call Venusport Medical," he said…

AS soon as the rubber-clad Medical examiners had finished prodding him, asking questions, and poking needles into him, Kim pulled on his lucite helmet, opened the filter-valve, and let himself into the ship's airlock. As the outer portal swung open, he dived headfirst out the opening and splashed into the soft, clinging mud.

He rolled onto his back and wiped the mud off his helmet.

He could hear the faint, shuddering blasts of gunfire down at the far end of the field, now. None of it sounded near him. No sparkling beams hissed over his head. Satisfied, he scrambled up on his hands and knees and went clawing through the deep mud toward the looming bulk of a nearby space freighter. Once there, he climbed to his feet. His body, clad only in brief shorts and gun-belt, was plastered with stinking mud. His helmet filter cut out the stink.

He went trudging off in the ankle-deep slime, sometimes sinking to his hips, his eyes searching warily among the dense cluster of big spacecraft hulls.

It began to rain. This was winter at Venusport; the rainy season. The rain came down in shimmering, blue-green curtains from the darkening mists above. Water swirled over the top of the mud and wispy clouds of white steam arose. The dense deluge washed his helmet sparkling clean in seconds, sluiced the layer of mud from his body. His skin smarted and stung from the impact of the raindrops. But he was thankful for the cover the rain afforded him.

It took him an hour of searching to find the *Voodoo*. There was no mistaking her when he did find her—he knew every bulge, scratch, and tarnish of her worn hull-plates. She stood alone, untended among the big, crowding ships.

He entered the airlock, warily, and stalked through her cool interior, his gun drawn and ready. She was empty, but the fuel-tanks were full and her provision-stores were well stocked. He pulled out her logbook and studied it with interest.

Then he left her and moved stealthily through the pouring, murmuring rain in the direction of the Venusport dome. The muttering boom of beams striking and disintegrating their targets sounded far off, muffled and unreal. He wondered if the rebels would succeed in infiltrating the Space Fleet lines under cover of the rain—but they'd probably had the chance, before now, and failed.

The flickering of the force-screen protecting the Venusport dome stopped him short of the field's edge. Several ships lay within the screen's protection—most of them, he noted with disgust, were official craft. He turned aside to the concrete pillbox entrance to one of the underground cargo tunnels that ran beneath the field.

Passing through the airlock, he removed his helmet and descended the long stairway to the broad, rock-walled corridor with its swiftly moving cargo ramp. He jumped onto the ramp and was borne rapidly toward the domed city. The ramp slowed and curved into a huge, vault-like warehouse chamber stacked high with giant crates. He stepped off the ramp, passed unconcerned through throngs of muscular stevedores, and took an automatic lift to the upper levels.

The white-haired old man in the office behind the transparent wall labeled *Venusport Communications* was at least a hundred and twenty years old. He was dressed simply in a scant loin-string supported by a gun belt, and his lean, milk-white body was supple and muscular. The plate on his curving desk bore the name: Rene Moskowitz. He shook hands cordially and waved Kim to a chair.

"That was a neat bit of juggling you did, bringing the *Eohippus* in," he praised in a quiet, gentle voice. "Few teams ever wiggle past old Shadow Peak without knocking a chunk off her. Now, what can we do for you, Mr. Rothman?"

Kim grinned good-naturedly. "So you know I'm a pirate, eh?"

"There's been some talk," Moskowitz conceded. "Understand you're after the sacred metal of the Gep Tzong."

"The—Gep Tzong?" Kim echoed questioningly.

"Name of those Toad Men up in the Misty Mountains," Moskowitz explained. "They've been making raids on the outlying plantations, carrying off equipment. Which is why the free settlers were so anxious to get the new equipment we were holding here. Earth wouldn't authorize us to release it, though—so the free settlers are trying to take it."

"You sound like you don't blame them, much," Kim remarked critically.

"I'm not sayin'." Moskowitz grinned with calm wisdom.

Kim nodded approvingly. "What I want," he said, "is this: you keep a file on the routine radio checks made by ships en route to or from Venus. I want to know about the voyage of one Yin Chao-Tang, aboard the scout cruiser *Voodoo*—"

"I don't need to search any file for that one," Moskowitz replied, grinning. "This Chao-Tang made radio contact with us on routine check until he was about ten days out from Earth—then he quit. The *Voodoo* came in here about two weeks ago with a three-man crew: a man and two women—"

"Oriental?" Kim asked sharply.

Moskowitz shook his head, chuckling. "There's a large Oriental faction here, though. You might check their religious leaders—"

Kim rose abruptly. "Thanks."

"Not at all, son."

THERE were four small amphitheaters on Level Two. On the glassite front walls were the symbols of each: the Cross of Jesus, the Star of David, the Star of Mohammed, and the Statue of Buddha. There were other temples elsewhere in the city, but Kim found these four together.

In the small office behind the transparent wall bearing the Star of David sat a tall, gray-haired man. On the curving desk before him was a nameplate: Rabbi Jacobi Rosenblum. He rose, rustling his simple, gray robe, and extended his hand as Kim entered. "Good afternoon, Mr. Rothman. Sit down."

Kim shook hands and sat down. "I need help," he said, "and I think you will help me."

"If I can," Rosenblum replied, sinking back behind his desk. He leaned forward, intently. "Kim Rothman, a space pirate, has arrived in Venusport with a scientific expedition. He has agreed to guard the expedition with his guns in return for the sacred radioactive metal of the Gep Tzong—is that true?"

"There is scientific basis for doubt that any such metal exists," Kim replied guardedly. "It's like the Amerindian legends of the golden cities that sent Spanish conquistadors to their death in the deserts. The purpose of the expedition is to prove whether there are Toad Men or Gep Tzong as you call them—if there are, who they are, and what they are..."

Rosenblum frowned dubiously. "Several thousand Gep Tzong have raided the outlying plantations, Mr. Rothman. They exist, well enough..."

"Who said so?"

Rosenblum practically bit his tongue with surprise. "Ah! There you have a point. The plantation owners claimed they were raided, and the delicate situation here at Venusport turned into an armed revolt. But there is no one to profit by the revolt—it has halted our exports to Earth. Even if the rebels win, it will stop further supplies coming from Earth. And the Earth corporations have no interest here—it is forbidden by law."

Kim waved his hand in an airy gesture. "All right, that's your problem. My concern is the expedition for the Biochemical Research Department. Do you realize that if there are native Venusians, we're actually invaders of this planet?"

"Eh? But—but that's absurd. Many of us were born here—" The tall Rabbi was profoundly shocked. "But of course, of course—it is still their planet. Still, there do not seem to be many of them—savages, too—perhaps, then, an agreement—"

"That," Kim pointed out, flatly, "is the purpose of the expedition I'm serving. Now, do we understand each other?"

Rosenblum took a deep breath and let it out, slowly. "I believe we do, Mr. Rothman," he affirmed. "So what is it that I can do for you?"

"Take me to the priesthood of the Oriental faction, here," Kim replied. "I am representing the family of Chao-Tang, of Earth."

Rosenblum pursed his lips. "I see," he said, then rose briskly. "Come along…"

They went out into the broad corridors. Venusport was a busy, thriving metropolis, abounding with merchants and shopkeepers and technical plant workers. Mingled with them were sturdy plantation owners and reptile hunters, garbed in suits of the sleek, blue-gray hide of the *ghrakko* dog. All of them, men and women, wore guns. The hunters carried their Chavez rifles easily in the crook of their arm.

Rosenblum led the way with a long, robe-flapping stride. "Business as usual," he explained of the crowds in the corridors. "You'd never know there were hostilities all around us, except that a few of the taverns have closed and you don't see many nondescript characters about. We had an influx of them before the revolt."

"Pirates?" Kim asked casually.

"A few," the Rabbi asserted. "Cutthroats and blackguards, mostly. All talking of the treasure of the Gep Tzong." He cast a speculative side-glance at Kim. "Someone with money could give your Department expedition some stiff competition…"

Kim nodded. "I'm aware of that."

Rosenblum was silent as they rode an escalator downward. Then, as they; reached the First Level, he turned quizzically. "Mind telling me why you came to me?"

Kim grinned sheepishly. "My parents were Jewish."

The Rabbi nodded. "I understand." He strode onward, briskly.

Kim followed him with a thoughtful scowl. There was something else, Kim realized suddenly, that Rosenblum might help him with—it wasn't easy for him to find words for it.

He stopped with grim decision and caught the Rabbi's arm. "I've got to ask you something," he said stiffly. "Something else—"

Rosenblum turned, smiling faintly. "Anything, Mr. Rothman…"

"There's a girl—" Kim instantly felt like a fool, but he couldn't stop. "My teammate," he explained. "She was born on Venus, but raised on Earth. She's—civilized—"

"Of course." Rosenblum nodded understandingly. "Her name?"

"Frances Freemont."

"She is Jewish?"

Kim shook his head. "No. Protestant, I think—I don't know—"

Rosenblum's smile broadened. "And you wish to marry her, of course. What is your religion, Kim Rothman?"

Kim shrugged. "What *is* religion? There are the planets, the Sun, the stars—the Universe—and us. How? Finding out how is science. But why? Wondering why, seeking answers in the laws of the Universe, seeing purpose and design—that's religion, isn't it?"

"The religion of the stars." Rosenblum nodded quietly. "There is its counterpart here on Venus. The swamp-jungle, the teeming life—wild, ferocious, but with purpose and design. And meaning. The religion of nature. And who is to deny that God's wisdom is revealed in His works?" He strolled on, hands clasped behind his back. "Some can find His wisdom in nature and the Universe; some can't. Those who can't come to us for spiritual guidance."

He lapsed into pensive silence for a moment, then turned and gazed at Kim, searchingly. "There is a recognized custom, here on Venus. When a man and woman come out of the wilderness wearing clothes from the same *ghrakko* skin, they are officially married. But Miss Freemont wouldn't know that, I suppose—"

Kim shook his head, miserably.

Rosenblum patted his shoulder.

"Before your expedition leaves, I shall speak to her," he promised softly. "I'm—I'm glad you asked me, Kim Rothman."

THE apartment they entered had no identifying mark or symbol on the outside. Within, in the silent gloom tainted with sweet incense, was a small, fat Oriental in a golden robe. He bowed low.

Rosenblum returned the bow. "Rabbi Jacobi Rosenblum," he introduced himself, then gestured to Kim. "Kim Rothman. He represents the family of Chao-Tang, of Earth."

The Oriental bowed again. Rosenblum slapped Kim's shoulder affectionately and took his leave.

The Oriental priest faced Kim and spoke in a soft, reedy voice. "What is your wish?"

"The brother of Yin Chao-Tang would wish to reclaim the body," Kim answered. "I can identify him."

"Come." The priest pushed aside a curtain and led Kim through a small doorway. They passed down a long, narrow corridor to its end, where the priest touched a stud that slid a panel aside. They entered a low vault-like room.

The body was stretched on a stone table. Most of the chest was blown away, but there was no mistaking the bald dome of the head, the thin features, and the white goatee.

"It is Yin Chao-Tang," Kim said.

The priest sucked his breath in, sharply. "Then the space pirates have not cheated us. It is well."

Kim knew what he meant. If an Oriental is killed in space, the body must be brought to its "cousins" on some planet for shipment home. If it isn't, the Oriental "cousins" demand satisfaction—which, in the case of murder, meant slow death for the murderer.

And this was a case of murder. "It is well," Kim agreed grimly.

CHAPTER EIGHT
Departure From Venusport

THE mud-cat threw mud and water fifty feet high from its broad, steel-flanged caterpillar treads as it came mushing and wallowing out across the spaceport field. The rain was coming down in a fine, blue-green haze and soaked the thick mud on the cat's armored sides so it dropped off in sticky blobs, revealing the rusted plates beneath with their red letters: Spaceport Repair.

Off in the distance somewhere, hidden by the rain, there were still the muffled, drumming explosions of gunfire.

But there was activity around the squat, ugly hull of the *Eohippus*. A huge tarpaulin had been stretched from her back out to supporting poles and guide-wires, forming a shelter alongside the ship that reached out to the metal hatchway of a big freight elevator. Gangs of helmeted stevedores were unloading crates and boxes from the ship's cargo locks, dragging them over to the freight elevator, and lowering them into the tunnels below the field.

The mud-cat splattered to a halt with a shrill whine of its turbines and Kim swung down from its tiny airlock. He waved the cat-driver off and went slogging through the mud toward the ship, noting several members of the expedition standing around watching the unloading. Kim waved to them and clambered up the short metal ladder to the ship's airlock.

Fran came running through the steel corridor within to meet him, just as he was tugging his helmet loose.

"Kim!" She leaped at him, hugged him, laughed and hugged him again. "I was so worried! Where've you been?"

"—Uh—out reclaiming my ship, the *Voodoo,*" he said, somewhat out of breath. Then he held her close, chuckling. "Blast it, Fran—I wasn't gone *that* long."

She struggled, pushed free, and held him back at arm's length, looking up at him, gravely. "What's this about the *Voodoo?*" she asked.

Kim's features sobered. "Yin Chao-Tang never reached Venus alive," he explained. "I've taken over the *Voodoo* and had Spaceport Repair weld a steel beam across her airlock. She'll be here when we want her again, or I'll know the reason why. Where are our prisoners?"

"MacSneary and that—that girl? Locked in their stateroom, I suppose."

Kim nodded, satisfied. "Any word from Dimitrios?"

"Not yet." She moved close to him, again.

"Better get back on the bridge, then." He kissed her quickly, swung her around, and spanked her bottom. She leaped back into the corridor with a pleased howl.

Kim turned aft, shaking his head and grinning. He'd really lose something if he ever lost Fran!

A studious-looking young man with a Chavez rifle across his arm stood before the locked stateroom door. He grinned as Kim approached. "How's it going, Mr. Rogers?" he asked pleasantly.

"It's Rothman, again," Kim told him. "I'm going in and speak to that space pirate in there as a space pirate. I'd rather not have you around."

The young man's features tightened and he stared hard at Kim for a moment. Then he shrugged indifferently. "I suppose it's all right." He hitched up his shorts and walked on down the corridor.

Kim pressed the auto-lock and slid back the door. His hand dropped to the butt of his right gun as he stepped into the stateroom.

Then he saw it wasn't necessary. Black Dog MacSneary was sprawled on the floor, his back against the far wall, and the girl was sitting on his lap, clutched in the embrace of his thick, hairy arms. She turned her head and glared up at Kim.

"Get outa here!" she snarled.

"Sorry," he said softly. "No more free meals and bunk for you two. On your feet, now, or I'll scorch your bottoms…"

The girl muttered a curse and turned back to MacSneary. The old pirate gave Kim his snaggle-toothed grin and laughed harshly. "'Smatter, sonny-boy? Want us to go runnin' free and eatin' people?" Then he threw back his head and filled the chamber with thunderous laughter.

Kim smiled mirthlessly. "You almost fooled me with that, Mac—but not quite," he said. "Sweetie-pie, here, was a little too anxious to get back in your lap for me to believe you'd chewed up her girlfriends…"

"Oh, go blow!" the girl sneered into MacSneary's beard.

"I've seen cannibal madness in people before," Kim went on, gazing down at MacSneary and ignoring the girl. "I got curious about this. I found out a lot."

MacSneary was listening, now. His cold, hard eyes were squinting narrowly. "You found out *what?*" he asked scornfully.

"After you escaped the Space Fleet in that lifeboat," Kim told him gently, "you heaved to on the Earth-Venus lane and waited for us. But then you picked up the routine radio-check of Yin Chao-Tang, in the *Voodoo*. You knew the Chao Tang family was in on the expedition; you thought Yin was a part of it. You hailed him, same as you did us—"

The girl had been staring up, her mouth widening. "He knows!" she gasped.

"But Yin tried to make a crooked deal," Kim continued. "You didn't like it. But Yin had money and he had the *Voodoo*. So you shot him, loaded his body back aboard the *Voodoo*, and sent three of your crew on ahead to Venus. You and Sweetie-pie, here, remained to bait us with that cannibalism deal—"

"You dirty scum!" the girl suddenly shouted at MacSneary. "And you *starved* me—"

The pirate's big paw struck her on the temple, knocking her completely out of his lap onto the deck. "Shut up!" he snapped gutturally.

"It was a neat scheme," Kim said, grinning. "A nice, big practical joke. We arrive in Venusport and start spreading the word about you stuffing yourself on your women, and then your women step out and make us the laughing-stock of Venus. Meanwhile, you've lined up as many henchmen here as you can buy—and the rest would only laugh at me if I tried to hire 'em—"

MacSneary rolled his eyes and shrugged comically. "Nothing ventured, nothing gained. And now, I presume you want us to take our leave of this little—ahem—love nest?" His rough tones mocked Kim. The girl stirred and moaned on the deck, then sat up. Both men ignored her.

"Clear out," Kim ordered distinctly.

MacSneary heaved a regretful sigh. "Ah, well—come along, Poodles..." He put a thick arm around the girl, climbed to his feet, and lifted her bodily off the deck. He half-carried, half-dragged her through the door and down the corridor. Kim followed them, grimly.

MacSneary turned around when they reached the airlock chamber. "You're really making a mistake, you know."

"Am I?" Kim asked lightly.

The girl pulled herself erect beside MacSneary, a dark red bruise on the side of her face. MacSneary shook loose from her irritably. "Of course," he spoke to Kim. "You're going to have plenty of competition getting that Venusian treasure. You will need all the help you can get. We ought to be friends, Mr. Rothman—not enemies."

Kim pointed to the stack of boxed helmets in the corner of the room. "Get your helmets on…" He fastened his own helmet, deftly.

The girl moved quickly, snatching a helmet and plunking it down over her head. Kim noticed that her body was dirt-smeared, unwashed, and clad only in a ragged strip of cloth. MacSneary merely shrugged and moved leisurely, taking his own good time about putting on a helmet.

"Snap it up!" Kim told him, opening the airlock portal for the girl.

"Of course, of course…" MacSneary followed them into the airlock, waited patiently until the inner door was sealed and the outer door opened, then turned to Kim. The girl jumped immediately to the slimy mud.

"You realize, of course, this means war between us," the old pirate said softly.

Kim took a step backward, then planted a hard kick squarely in the middle of the pirate's dirty red trunks. MacSneary went hurtling out of the airlock, headfirst, and smacked into the mud.

The girl stood over him, staring down at him, blankly.

MacSneary climbed slowly, laboriously to his feet. "Come, Poodles," he said, taking the girl's arm. "We aren't appreciated here."

They went stumbling and lurching off across the field. The girl looked back, once, and stuck her tongue out at Kim.

DIMITRIOS had radioed Fran by the time Kim returned to the bridge. The scientist wanted them both to meet him in the Governor's office.

Fran belted a gun onto her thigh, donned a helmet, and they rode a tunnel ramp into the city. The Governor's office was on Level Fifteen, a sumptuous, vault-like suite of rooms. Dimitrios came hurrying to meet them in the glittering anteroom.

"Trouble..." the scientist muttered cryptically. "Follow me—the Governor's waiting to receive us."

As they followed him across the room to a tall pair of ivory portals, Kim noted with a faint smile the blue-uniformed Space Fleet guards standing stiffly at attention around the room. The Governor of Venusport certainly wasn't taking any chances, what with armed rebels raising the hue and cry about his very doors.

A set of almost perfect twins in snappy blue uniforms knocked their heels together. The two tall, ivory portals swung sedately open. A soft chime rang from somewhere within. Then Dimitrios, Kim, and Fran walked in. They strode across the deep, ebony pile carpet toward a monstrosity of a desk in bright ivory.

Behind the desk sat a hard-faced man in a brilliantly beribboned uniform. Beside the desk sat another man also in uniform but less colorfully beribboned. The man beside the desk rose, clicked his heels, and bowed. "Gentlemen," he said. "His Excellency, Vallisanovitch Serkov, Governor of Venus..."

Serkov gave them a thin-lipped smile. "My Aide-de-Camp, Commander Hans Kruger of the Space Fleet. Sit down, Gentlemen." His eyes flicked over Fran's slender figure. "And ladies," he added softly.

They sat down. Commander Kruger of the Space Fleet sat down. Governor Serkov leaned his elbows on his desk. "I will address my remarks to all three of you," he said bluntly. "You have placed me in a rather ticklish position with your proposed expedition. However, you have authorization from Earth. So I can't stop you—"

"*Stop* us?" Fran exclaimed.

Serkov silenced her with a curt wave of his hand. "Kindly let me finish." He leaned back in his chair and stared at them for a moment. "I have already given authorization to a group of free settlers to go out in an expedition to attack these Gep Tzong animals. I have allowed twenty mud-cats and drivers to leave Venusport and join this expedition. Its purpose is to drive those toad-like ape beasts back into the mountains.

"You people from the Biochemical Research Department are under the assumption that these Gep Tzong are intelligent creatures. Nothing could be farther from the truth. Our settlers have reported seeing the beasts and killing them on sight. They are beasts, similar to Earth's apes, nothing else…

"There has been considerable rabble-rousing around here with a fantastic tale of a sacred treasure and villages and temples in the mountains—utter rot! The rebel group has claimed that the Gep Tzong beasts have been raiding to get machinery, which is nothing more than a bald lie concocted to cover up their own shiftlessness. If they'd taken proper care of their machinery, they'd still have it. No Gep Tzong beasts stole it, I assure you."

"I was afraid of this," Dimitrios said coldly. "Your Excellency, the Department does not concede that the Gep Tzong are beasts—but neither do we claim they are intelligent. It is the purpose of our expedition to *find out* if they're intelligent—"

"Nevertheless," Serkov retorted, "the rebel group has used that lie as a propaganda basis for their armed rebellion against the government of Venusport. As I said, I cannot stop your expedition. But neither can I spare any troops to protect your expedition if you're foolish enough to go out in the Gep Tzong country…"

The scientist's face twitched into a pained smile. "I'm surprised that I should have to say this, but you aren't going to find out anything about the Gep Tzong by sending armed expeditions out to kill them."

Serkov snorted. "You *are* fools, aren't you? Very well—that's your affair. But I must also add that any action on the part of your pirate cohort, here—" He flicked a finger in Kim's direction. "—Any action by him against the other expedition, which I have duly authorized, and I will see to it that he is arrested, tried, and executed within a week."

Kim grinned mirthfully. "Sure you can spare the men for it?"

Serkov's face assumed the gray color of a chunk of granite. "That is the reason—the only reason—you were invited to this discussion, Mr. Rothman. I warn you that I am a man of my word."

Kim nodded in mocking agreement. "And this other expedition—it's being formed by the—uh 'free settlers outside the attacking rebels' lines?"

"Yes," Commander Kruger spoke up, nodding. "The rebels allowed our mud-cats through to join that expedition."

Kim's eyes narrowed thoughtfully. "When was this?"

"Why—two weeks ago…" Kruger's brows went up. "Why do you ask?"

"Any reason they haven't left, already?"

"Takes time to organize an expedition, I suppose." Kruger shrugged perplexedly.

"It doesn't take two weeks!" Dimitrios exclaimed shrewdly.

"Uh huh," Kim grunted. "And I'll bet they're waiting for us to start out, first."

"Eh?" Governor Serkov looked vaguely uneasy. "Why would they do that?"

Kim chuckled. "So we can show them the way to the Gep Tzong village, of course. And—to the sacred treasure."

Serkov snorted. "Hogwash! There is no—"

"Let *me* finish…" Kim interjected harshly. "Do you know anything at all about who financed that armed expedition of so-called 'free settlers'? Do you know who's leading it?"

Serkov smiled thinly. "Do you?"

Kim nodded. "Black Dog MacSneary. Get your Fleet Intelligence agents out to check on the corpse of Yin Chao-Tang being held by the local Orientals, and who delivered it to them under what circumstances. You're going to find, Your Excellency, that you've already been taken by a pirate."

They waited while Serkov checked. It took most of an hour, but when the reports came trickling in, Serkov wasn't pleased. He got up and began pacing the deep pile carpet.

It became readily apparent, from the reports, that MacSneary's henchmen had succeeded in organizing an armed expedition of Venusport's toughest killers, roustabouts, and thieves with the Governor's complete, ignorant permission. Furthermore, that expedition was now encamped outside the lines of the attacking rebels, out of reach of the Governor and his Space Fleet troops.

Serkov shook his head, stubbornly. "There's nothing to be done about it now," he said. "Perhaps they will still drive those Gep Tzong beasts back into the mountains. Dr. Dimitrios—" He swung to the scientist. "I do not think it advisable for your expedition to leave Venusport at this time."

"Sorry," Dimitrios smiled faintly. "You can't stop us— remember?"

Serkov stalked over and stood looking down at Dimitrios. "Please understand my position, sir!" the Governor said gruffly. "If you found out that those Gep Tzong were intelligent, why—why I'd lose the moral support of everyone inside the dome of this city."

"You'd lose more than that," Dimitrios exclaimed musingly. "You would lose Venus…"

"Eh?" Serkov started. "How's that?"

The scientist smiled up at him.

"If the Gep Tzong are intelligent Venusian natives, Your Excellency—why, Venus belongs to them…"

"What?" Serkov gaped foolishly. "Why—why, that's preposterous!"

Dimitrios shook his head. "I'm afraid the Department—and the Earth government—would have a slightly different view. They would probably be very anxious for you to put down this rebel uprising as soon as possible. Poor example to the natives, you know."

Serkov's eyes widened as the implication became clear. "Then—in *that* case—I'll win, either way. Yes…how soon can your expedition be ready to leave?"

Dimitrios struggled to keep from laughing. "As soon as we can line up our mud-cats and get loaded," he answered crisply.

"Then get at it," Serkov ordered. "I'll send a parleying group out to talk the rebels into letting your group through their lines—about time I started parleying with them, anyhow. This fighting's doing neither side any good." He stalked back behind his desk and slumped down. "Gentlemen, the planet Venus has been nothing but trouble to mankind ever since the first expedition tried to reach here."

Dimitrios, rising, missed part of the Governor's last statement. The scientist turned, frowning. "Expedition? Another one?"

"The—uh—first one," Serkov explained hastily. "The *S. S. Starling III,* I think it was, tried to reach Venus a hundred and seventy years ago. And it was another hundred years before they finally succeeded in reaching this hell-hole and planting a colony on it."

"Hmmm," Dimitrios sounded out. "Well, we'd best get to work, Your Excellency—"

"Naturally."

"Good day." The scientist turned and stalked disdainfully out, Kim and Fran following in his footsteps. " 'Excellency,' is he?" Dimitrios snorted, as they passed through the outer anteroom. "A diplomat the Earth government was probably glad to get rid of, that's what he is. So they sent him out here."

"That's usually the way it is," Kim remarked bitterly.

THERE was, in Venusport, a society known as the Dark Watch. They were called dark because, originally, most of them had been dark a few generations earlier. They were descendants of early Negro settlers from Earth. The peculiar radiology of Venus had gone to work on them through three or four rapid generations—as children were born in rapid succession on a frontier and had changed their normally dark complexion to a color resembling the golden smoothness of rich butter-cream. It was about as near as they had come to the near-albino whiteness that had affected other settlers' children.

And they were called the Watch because the demands of the frontier had considerably altered their status. The early Negro settlers had shipped out as unskilled workers. Their descendants were the best technicians in Venusport, noted for their mechanical wizardry; they were the maintenance squads who kept watch over the domed city's mechanisms, and were famed as mechanics and cat-drivers. The latter were well acquainted, through extensive travelling, with most of the known region of the planet.

Their rise in status, of course, had nothing to do with the radiological affects of the planet on skin pigmentation. Their skill was due solely to the extensive training school they had organized.

Indeed, with one of their members, race had been no drawback whatsoever. This was Mr. Throwback Samson.

"I was nicknamed Throwback," Mr. Samson explained, introducing himself, "because that's just what I am—a throwback to my great-granddaddy!" And he flashed white, even teeth in a broad grin.

Kim gaped up at him, speechlessly.

They were standing on a tunnel floor. The moving cargo ramp had been stopped and big, powerful mud-cats were rumbling up on it from Venusport. A short distance ahead, a freight elevator was accepting the heavy cats one at a time and lifting them to the surface of the spaceport field. People were clamoring over the steel backs of the cats, shouting excitedly to one another over the deep rumble of turbine engines.

The man standing before Kim was a good six inches taller than he was. Moreover, Throwback Samson was solid muscle—broad shoulders, deep chest, and tremendous, rippling sinews. A wide belt about his thighs supported a loincloth, a holstered Maxim, and the curved, razor-edged scimitar Venus settlers preferred as a swamp-knife.

And he was certainly a throwback. He was the blackest man Kim had ever seen in his life. He was like a huge, grinning black shadow in the dim tunnel light. The whites of his eyeballs and the sparkling line of his teeth seemed to glow benevolently from his black, handsomely molded face.

Kim took a deep breath. "You're the man the Dark Watch recommended as a guide?" he asked, keeping his voice casual.

A deep chuckle rumbled up from Samson's chest, blending with the engine rumble of the big cats beside them. "I know every square inch of the known regions of Venus, plus a lot the maps say is unexplored," he stated firmly. "And not by accident, either—I've taken mud-cats through some of the worst terrain on this planet. Dragged 'em out of salt-mires with every bolt on 'em half-corroded, tuned 'em up in the middle of the swamp and made 'em purr like kittens. Had to."

Kim grinned. "In other words, you know your way around," he taunted good-naturedly. "But, listen—there may be fighting—"

Throwback dropped one eyebrow in a pained frown. "I see you haven't been on Venus long. Since when wasn't there a fight?"

"All right," Kim nodded. "As guide and scout, you'll ride Dimitrios' cat at the head of the column. But we aren't pulling out until morning, and I'd feel better if you could do something for us in the meantime. Can you get through the rebel lines?"

Throwback laughed. "At night, I'm the one man who can get *anywhere*. Why, though? Want me to slip out and check on that outlaw expedition?"

"That's the idea. Find out what they're doing, how many they are, what arms they have, if you can manage it. But don't take any more risks than you have to."

"Don't worry," Throwback countered. "I probably know more about that than you do."

Kim pursed his lips and nodded, grinning. "You probably do, at that. Don't be gone longer than midnight, though—we're pulling out early."

"Midnight it is." Throwback gave a brief nod and moved with long, swinging strides toward the freight elevator. He turned and called back, "If I don't show up, Rothman, don't come after me. You would never make it—and I won't be alive…"

He picked up a helmet near the tunnel wall, clamped it over his shoulders, and rode up on the elevator with a rumbling mud-cat.

FOURTEEN men and nine women, all scientists of one sort or another. Heavy cases of scientific equipment. Twenty-five big mud-cats with their golden-skinned drivers. Plus arms, ammunition batteries, food supplies, distilled water, emergency oxygen tanks, medical supplies, turbine fuel, and spare parts for the cats. An expedition on Venus was no small matter.

The big cats crawled around in the mud to form a tight circle as they were lifted to the spaceport field. A sputtering arc light was rigged in the middle of the circle, giving them light to work by. It was shielded by the cats from any spying eyes out on the far end of the field, where bright flashes and muffled blasts indicated the fighting was still going on.

The mud-cats were huge, metal behemoths looming up in the wet, misty blackness of the night. Kim walked around the inside of their perimeter, beating his fist into his palm and scowling through the cracks between them at the fathomless darkness. It was three hours past midnight.

Fourteen men, nine women in the expedition. Twenty-five drivers with the cats. Forty-eight people, plus Dimitrios, Fran, himself, and Throwback Samson, which made fifty-two.

Explorers on an alien planet, with a travelling laboratory that had to be fought, pushed, and driven across that planet. Going out to make peace with an alien species of intelligent life that had already proven itself unfriendly, ferocious…

People stood in groups beside their cats, talking. People scrambled up over the shadowy backs of the cats, checking and securing the cables that held the great mounds of equipment lashed down under heavy tarpaulins. People like Kim, himself, wearing transparent filter-helmets over their heads, garbed now in the drab brown suits that covered them from neck to feet with a thin, tightly woven fabric that no insect's stinger could penetrate. Pistols and swamp-knives belted about their hips, Chavez rifles slung over their shoulders.

All of them there, now. All ready. Dimitrios had received the Governor's message that the rebels would let them through their lines at a specified time. And that time would arrive in another hour.

And all of them were there, ready—except one. Throwback Samson hadn't come back.

Kim stamped around the circle of cats, scowling and peering between them. Three hours past midnight and still no Samson. Kim felt a gnawing conscience that tore at his guts. Had he sent that big, handsome black man out to his death? If he had, by all the little Satans in Hell, Black Dog MacSneary would die slowly, inch by inch...

Kim paused in his nervous stride, just once. He stood looking across the lighted circle to where Fran stood leaning against the tall, mud splattered flank of the cat they would ride. Before Fran, seated on a chunk of rock, was the tall, robed figure of Rabbi Rosenblum. His features were quietly intent within his helmet, and he was speaking calmly. And Fran was listening with a blush that set her cheeks aglow and a sparkle that shone in her eyes like scintillating flames. Her lips were curved in a soft, sweet smile...

Kim whirled and resumed his pent-up stride, slamming his fist against the steel side of a cat and scowling out into the dark night with a muttered curse.

He reached the narrow gap between two cats and slid to a halt, staring. The night out there was still a wet, misty blackness. And the huge, black figure standing there was almost invisible. Only the grin and the faint gleam of the helmet stood out.

"*Samson!*" Kim gasped. "Blast it man, you—"

A deep chuckle answered him, and Samson strode in past the cats with a supple, silent grace that gave an illusion that he came flowing out of the darkness. "I learned the time we would depart from the rebels," he explained gently. "They're sure a talkative bunch, out there."

"Let's go find Dimitrios and hear your report." Kim turned and led the way over to the scientist's cat. "You've had me in a stew, fella."

"I wanted to check on that MacSneary gang's movements up to the latest possible moment," Samson replied with a casual lightness. "Around midnight, they must've learned the way the rebels were going to let us drive out of here. They posted gunners along the route with the idea of knocking off some of our cats, but when the rebel boss heard about it, he went over and shooed 'em out. Said he wasn't going to get his war messed up with no private squabbles on the side."

Kim heaved a sigh of relief. "I was afraid they'd try something like that."

"They won't, now," Samson said, chuckling. "Not unless they want to take on the whole rebel forces."

Dimitrios saw the two men approaching through the glassite blister of the cat's cockpit. The scientist emerged, helmeted, through the tiny airlock and dropped to the ground to meet them. Kim made the introductions and Samson shook hands with him, cordially.

"Rothman said I'd ride with you," the tall scout said.

Dimitrios nodded. "Glad you'll be along, too, Samson. We'll certainly need you. Now, about that other group—"

"They've got around sixty men, all armed," Samson reported. "That includes the cat-drivers, though, who'll stick to their cats and have little to do with any private fights—

which leaves about forty gunners to worry us. They have twenty cats fully provisioned for a long trip, plus six *ghrakko* dogs—"

"*Ghrakko* dogs?" Dimitrios blurted in surprise.

Samson nodded with an expression of disgust. "Some fool out there decided they'd buy their *ghrakko* mounts here. *Ghrakkos* are terrified by the swamps, and when they get them out in that green hell with those roaring mud-cats, those *ghrakko* dogs will go mad and tear their riders to pieces. I've seen it happen too often."

Dimitrios grinned dourly. "Well…that's their worry. You've done a good job, Mr. Samson. We'll be pulling out in twenty minutes." He turned to Kim. "We'll be three days going through the Low Swamps, Rothman. The fourth day, we'll climb the High Slopes to Delaray's Mill—buy our *ghrakko* dogs there. From then on, we'll be in unexplored country. Up through the Misty Mountains and down into the passes or valleys or whatever we find beyond. Got that?"

"Right," Kim said. I'd like to make a suggestion, though."

"Yes?"

"Samson reports that MacSneary's gang has tried to lay ambush along our route out of here, but the rebels wouldn't allow it," Kim spoke grimly. "Pirates, though, have a tendency to ignore warnings, so there may be a few pot-shots at us anyhow—"

Dimitrios frowned worriedly. "What's your suggestion?"

"Let my cat lead the column out of here," Kim replied. "If there's any ambush, I'll spot it. If there isn't, we'll go on through. Once my cat is clear of Venusport, I'll swing around and stand guard while you lead the rest of the column on past. Then I'll fall in behind and keep watch on our rear."

"Good idea," Samson approved instantly.

"Go ahead," Dimitrios seconded. "Samson and I will fall in behind you." He swung toward the circle of cats and raised his voice to a shout. *"All right everybody! Mount up! March order!"*

Kim whirled and ran swiftly toward his own cat.

"I'M Winnetka," the driver said, grinning, as the cat's turbine came to life with a muffled growl. "Winnetka Jones, that is."

"Glad to know you, Jones," Kim replied, clamping a Chavez rifle into the turret-mounts in the roof of the cockpit blister. "Soon as she's warmed up, pull out. We're leading the column out of Venusport."

"Oh-oh," Jones murmured, gazing back and up at the mounted rifle. "I hope you're a good shot with that thing. If anybody starts shooting at us, hang on—I'll have this cat skinning itself all over Venus."

"He's a good shot, all right," Fran consoled Jones. She looked up at Kim, gravely. "Trouble, darling?"

"Maybe." Kim strapped himself to the bucket seat in the turret. "If there is, we'll be ready for it."

"All set?" Jones spoke sharply over the rising thunder of the turbines.

"All set!" Fran and Kim chorused.

The cat bit its flanged treads into the mud and lurched forward.

"Fran!" Kim shouted above the roar. "Man the searchlights! Keep 'em sweeping all around us!"

Fran twisted in her seat to obey. Three searchlight beams shot out at opposing angles from the mud-cat, as she manipulated the lever handles. Jones studied the map tacked to its board beside his control panel, peered ahead through his periscope slit, and altered the cat's direction toward the far end of the field. There was one certain path they had to follow through the rebel lines...

Kim looked back over the top of the lurching, roaring cat to see the other cats swinging into a long column behind them, like huge, ferocious monsters charging across the field, flinging mud up from their terrible claws. He pulled the lever that turned the turret around and gazed ahead into the inky blackness to the long line of tiny, blazing flashes that was rapidly approaching. Jones would have to hit their pre-determined path through that No Man's Land exactly, or they would have their cat blasted out from under them.

He did. They toppled off the edge of the level spaceport field and went charging down a shallow, crater-pocked draw. The bright flashes of exploding beams swept past at a good distance on either side of them. The cat's roving lights picked out mud-caked, blue-uniformed Space Fleet troopers clutching rifles and crouching behind their force-screen projector shields. Then the gully flattened out to a small plain that was torn and gashed to a hellish rubble. Then they bounded over a slight rise and roared past crouching figures of mud-splattered, half-naked rebel troops.

Another figure, an armed rebel standing erect, loomed before them, waving them to the left. Jones hauled the big cat around, spraying the rebel with mud, and they went thundering along a smooth, winding road. Settlers' huts, sealed prefab domes, began to appear on either side of the road. They were through the battle zone, now, driving on through the outer suburbs of Venusport. Kim checked his rifle and watched, tensely, as the searchlight beams played over the dark, silent huts. They thundered onward.

At twenty-yard intervals, the other cats followed them.

They roared past the last prefab dome and struck the muddy deep-rutted lane beyond. Giant blue fronds rose from glistening, black pools of water on either side of them. The cat bounced and shuddered over buried logs in the softer, shallow holes in the lane. It curved around and went up the steep shoulder of a black, lava-coated hill.

"Swing off and stop at the crest of this hill!" Kim shouted. Jones nodded mutely. Then, with a merry grin, he struck a switch that cut in the exhaust mufflers, and the turbines' roar faded to a deep, throbbing rumble.

"Sometimes loud noise can sure unnerve anybody trying to take a shot at you," he remarked calmly.

Kim stared down at him, then muttered a pleased oath.

As the purplish fronds dropped away and they crawled up the steep shoulder of the hill, Kim motioned Fran to douse their lights. He gazed back down the way they had come, counting the lights of the other cats. All twenty-five were still rolling. He gave a sigh of relief and loosened his seat straps.

Steel treads champing at the flinty soil, the cat hauled itself up on the crest of the hill and spun around to the side of the trail. Morning light was painting the dense cloud-blanket overhead a deep, shadowy blue, which brightened to a blazing green glow off near the invisible horizon. There were dim, gray shadows of giant mountains etched within the mists— towering, flat-topped chimney peaks rising many miles into the cloud-shrouded heavens.

And below was the slick, brown scum of the Low Swamps, patterned with broad patches of dark blue ferns, spotted with large islands of dense, black swamp jungle. In the misty distance, other islands were dimly visible—islands of jagged, volcanic cones that spouted red glares of molten rock and poisonous fumes into the clouds.

And up the narrow trail, curving around the shoulder of the hill, came the roaring, lurching monsters from Earth. The big, steel mud-cats snarling up out of the night's gloom, bulging humps of supplies and equipment lashed to their high backs, cockpit blisters agleam. Kim caught the wave of

Dimitrios' hand as his cat went thundering past; then the others followed, leaping, jolting, roaring.

The domed city of Venusport was lost somewhere in the wall of mists behind them.

CHAPTER NINE
The Gep Tzong Country

KIM sat cross-legged on a high ledge. The ledge was up on the brush-choked flank of a peak that disappeared into the orange-red clouds overhead. The clouds were so low they seemed almost close enough to touch.

Below was a deep gash between towering rock walls. The floor was crammed with jumbled boulders and twisted, gnarled trees.

The gash opened out on a broad valley. Beyond the valley were smaller peaks, like broken teeth, with orange clouds being torn to shreds on their black pinnacles by fierce hurricane winds.

Kim sat perfectly still, his helmet gleaming dully on his head, his rifle laid across his lap. He had been sitting there for the past two hours.

That kind of patience wasn't learned easily. Kim had learned it, in the past two weeks. He was toughened to it. His body beneath the drab brown coverall was solid and lean, with flat, hard muscles.

Before the muscles developed, there had been calluses; before the calluses, these had been aches and blisters. The pain of being slammed and jolted around in the steel confines of a lurching mud-cat. The strain of hard, bitter, merciless work.

They had crossed the swamplands, of Venus. Dimitrios, in the lead cat, shooting flame-jelly into the rough lane ahead to burn out the persistent, tough creeping-vines of the jungle.

The big cats wallowing ahead through the syrupy mud, plowing through the burning vegetation. The mud coated them thickly and was baked hard by the heat; it had to be chipped away in curved sheets from the transparent cockpit blisters. Swarms of angry insects rose from the fetid water, darkened the burning sky with their black cloud, and descended on the lumbering cats; the drivers snapped on the ultra-sonic sirens to frighten the insects away. At night, the convoy camped on high ground, while giant carnivores screamed and bellowed and crashed through the surrounding jungle.

Some days, it rained. The rain swept over them in solid curtains, and the water swirled up to the backs of the cats. But the cats rolled on. Occasionally, a cat would slip off the trail and sink into the bottomless mire; two other cats would be coupled together, then would haul the bogged cat back on the trail with their winch-cables. Then the convoy would move on.

Fran was right at home. She prepared the meals for Kim and Winnetka Jones, and spent the rest of her time educating them on the flora and fauna of Venus, the planet of her birth. Her knowledge was extensive, scientific, and accurate, so that even Jones listened. She pointed out the tracks of various animals to them, the swamp groves of certain plantation crops. There were certain plants on Venus that, when mashed to a pulp and processed, gave certain juices that were nutritious to Earthmen; the juices were used as a base for various synthetic foods, which made up most of the staple diet of the Venusian settlers. The water, too, was drinkable—when processed and distilled.

They climbed up out of the swamps, onto the slopes of the Misty Mountains. Three cats broke down as the going got tougher, slippery and rocky; the convoy stopped until the cats were repaired.

At their campsites, Kim became more and more attached to the tall scout, Throwback Samson. Kim was fairly certain that the other expedition would be somewhere behind them, following them in the trail they had blazed conveniently clear. But as nights passed, Kim and Throwback formed a habit of slipping out of the camp together, vanishing out into the stygian darkness and not returning until hours later. Once, when they returned, Throwback got an oily rag from one of the cat-drivers, handed it to Kim, and stood by with a silent grin as Kim wiped the dotted blood from the blade of his swamp-knife.

They were roaring, sliding, and spinning their tracks in the loose shale of a steep slope, one morning, when Dimitrios' voice blared from their radios: *"Cut your turbines and sit still. Remain in your cats and—above all—don't shoot!"*

And a huge, slate-gray reptile came waddling over the hill. Fifty feet high and two hundred feet along its spiked back, with small beady eyes in its bucket-shaped head and dragging itself along on huge, taloned claws. It spotted something—a purplish root—under one of the cats in the middle of the column, waddled up, and nudged the cat with its horny snout.

Somebody in a cat ahead got nervous. A Chavez beam lanced out and tore a boulder to smithereens behind the great beast.

It jerked its snout up and looked straight at the offending cat, speculatively.

"Stop firing," Dimitrios shouted into the radios. *"Don't fire again or it'll tear us all to pieces…"*

The monster lowered its snout toward the offensive cat and sniffed, very deliberately. Spouts of white steam shot from its nostrils. Then, apparently satisfied, it turned back to the other cat and nudged it gently. The great snout nudged the cat right over on its side, then a long, grayish tongue flicked out and tore the purple root right out of the ground.

Then, fed as well as satisfied, the reptile waddled sedately on down the slope, creating a minor avalanche of boulders.

The column wound up its turbines again and two cats winched the overturned cat back onto its treads. The convoy moved on.

They met the stocky, tough miller and his beautiful wife at Delaray's Mill, where the plantation crops were pulped and processed. The miller listened to their story, then shook his head. "Gep Tzong are animals," he said flatly. "Kill 'em on sight."

Dimitrios didn't like that. He called Kim aside in a private conference. Thereafter, it was decided, the expedition would move straight into the Gep Tzong country, in broad daylight, without any show of furtiveness or hesitation. The Gep Tzong had been attacked by unthinking settlers and were undoubtedly in an angry mood; any sign of craftiness or guile would probably bring an immediate attack down on the expedition. A forthright approach would have the best chance of bringing them down for a talk, instead of a massacre.

They bought six *ghrakko* mounts for scouting purposes at Delaray's Mill, and moved on. A week later, they were deep in the Misty Mountains—and in unexplored country.

Then Throwback found the webbed tracks.

"War party," he had said, glumly. "Marching in files. Soldiers."

SOMETHING moved on the jumbled floor far below. Kim shifted his rifle forward and flattened on the top of the ledge.

Like a tiny, crawling insect, a *ghrakko* dog came loping up into the deep gash from the valley beyond. Gradually, as it approached, Kim discerned the rider sitting atop the grotesque hump of its shoulders. A tall figure garbed in drab brown. Throwback Samson.

Kim climbed to his feet, slung the rifle over his shoulder, and scrambled down from the ledge. He walked back to a sleek, blue-gray *ghrakko* dog standing in the dense brush nearby, its jawful of fanged teeth strapped shut by the muzzling bridle. It dropped to its knees as he tugged the reins, and he climbed up into the hard saddle on its shoulder-hump. Then it scrambled up and picked its way down the narrow trail on the steep face of the cliff.

Webbed tracks meant the Gep Tzong. And two men had said the Gep Tzong were intelligent. The last one—Du Bois Thompson—had described the twenty years he had lived among them as a captive. In his carefully written report, he had told of their village far back in the Misty Mountains, of their greenish, toad-like appearance, of their rites and legends.

Their legends had the same savage bloodthirstiness of any tribe of barbarians on Earth. They believed they were descendants of a group of gods who had come down from the mountaintops and built a temple. Those gods had placed the sacred metal in the temple to guard it, had given birth to the first children of the Gep Tzong, and had died soon afterward—all but one. There was one who could not speak, and he had built fire and taught the first children. He was tall and thin and was a great god. But he had died.

And when DuBois Thompson was captured, he had been tall and thin. But he spoke. So they cut out his tongue and made him a god. And he had seen the tall, black tower of their temple, but they would not let him enter it because the sacred metal would kill him. Finally, he had fashioned a makeshift filter-mask and had escaped. He had walked back through the mountains and down the slopes and across the swamplands to Venusport.

Indeed, Kim thought grimly, *he too was a great god!*

Samson hailed him as his mount came scampering down the narrow cliff trail Kim reined it around on the rocky floor and went loping to meet the tall scout.

"Find anything?" he asked.

"Found plenty!" Samson replied emphatically. "Followed the tracks down into the valley we came through yesterday. MacSneary's column is camped down there."

"It was a scouting patrol?"

Samson shook his head. "My guess is it was a full-fledged war party. It missed us by only a couple of miles, coming through here before we arrived. From the looks of the tracks, it circled MacSneary's column, keeping out of sight and watching it. Then they held a council, probably decided there weren't enough of 'em to attack MacSneary's bunch, and they trotted on back into the mountains."

"Think they went back for reinforcements?"

"Right. Or they may stir up the whole tribe!" Samson scowled bitterly. "If they should come storming out of there, looking for blood, and should stumble onto our expedition instead of MacSneary's—" He left the rest unsaid.

Kim nodded thoughtfully. "We'd better get back and warn the others—though there may be a chance they were just curious—"

"Uh-uh," Samson refuted. "Maybe at first, but not any more. MacSneary's bunch spotted one of 'em—blasted him all over the landscape."

"That," Kim snapped, "is all we needed. Come on!"

They whipped their mounts on through the narrow gash that penetrated the wall of the mountains to another valley, higher up. The dogs were filmed with sweat and blowing through foam-flecked nostrils as they trotted out onto a gentle slope overlooking the valley. Sheer cliffs rose on all sides, vanishing into the orange mists overhead. The grass at this higher altitude, though, was more blue-green than purple, and the trees had rough brown trunks and greenish leaves instead of the soggy blue trunks and black fuzz-tops of the swamp jungles.

They took a winding ravine down the crumbling side of a deep pocket in the center of the valley, letting their dogs walk and catch their breath. The dogs' breathing was labored in the thin air of these higher valleys.

They zigzagged through a clump of tall green trees to a small, clear brook that came splashing out of the rocky cut of a small side-ravine when Kim suddenly drew rein. Samson pulled up beside him and they sat staring silently at the saddled *ghrakko* dog standing on the other side of the stream, its reins tied to a tree. It gazed back at them, placidly.

Samson voiced his question in one single word. "Who?"

"No telling," Kim replied softly. "Our camp isn't far below here. Maybe one of our people, or maybe MacSneary's got scouts out watching us, too."

"We'll see," Samson said.

They pulled their mounts back into the trees, dismounted, and tied them. Then the two men slipped silently back to the narrow cleft of the side-ravine. Cautiously, melting from shadow to shadow, gliding from bush to boulder to tree, rifles held ready. Samson pointed to the tracks of the other rider, followed them up into the narrow cleft where water gurgled merrily over the rocks. The two men went over rocks, too—belly-flat, like creeping lizards. They paused, listening, as a faint splash and rippling of water came from up ahead. Then they snaked forward into dense, tangled brush, inched through it on their elbows and toes, and reached out and parted the leaves very carefully.

They stiffened with amazement.

THE side-ravine had widened out to form a small, steep-walled hollow. A misty waterfall fell smoke-white from the far wall, hissing into a wide, deep pool. There was a small, rough boulder outcropping that jutted up in the center of the pool.

Fran Freemont was poised gracefully on the tip of the rock. She was a lovely, ivory-skinned figure with long, dark hair that rippled wetly down her back. She wore only a scant G-string and a bra—her brown coverall and gun-holster was folded neatly and placed over on the sandy edge of the pool. As she poised her lithe figure, she smiled with a complete, selfish pleasure.

And *she wore no helmet!*

Then, with a flash of ivory limbs, she arched out in a graceful dive and plunged neatly into the water, hardly making a splash.

And on the far side of the pool, squatting on the sands behind her, was a weird, toad-like creature with greenish-gray skin.

It had watched her, silently. Obviously without her knowledge that it was even there. It had followed her graceful dive with large, staring eyes. It was completely motionless, as though hypnotized with utter fascination.

Studying the Gep Tzong with a fascination of his own, Kim saw that it was actually a "he"—it had a thin, furry string about its, or rather, his loins. A cruelly barbed spear lay on the sand beside him. He looked much like a big greenish-gray toad. His arms and legs were thin, his hips narrow. But his chest was a huge, bulbous bladder that ballooned almost to his chin. His face was creased by a wide, thick-lipped mouth stretching from ear to ear, and two large, liquid eyes stared from either side of a short, stubby nose. And he was bald. Bald and a dark, glossy green.

Fran's head broke the surface and she rolled on her back, breathing easily.

The Toad Man opened his wide slit of a mouth and issued a long, whispering sigh.

At that moment, Fran saw him.

She dog-paddled gently, staring up at him. The Toad Man stared back at her. Neither of them uttered a sound.

Then, cautiously, the Toad Man moved. He inched down to the edge of the pond and extended one webbed foot toward the water. He stared at Fran, his foot poised. Then he dipped his foot into the water.

He jerked it out, instantly, and retreated back to his squatting position.

And Fran gave a soft, tinkling laugh.

That brought results. The Toad Man's lips twitched into a puzzled, sheepish expression.

"No sink," he said. Quite clearly, too.

Fran gasped. *"What?"*

The Toad Man stirred irritably. "You no sink!" he said.

"Well-l-l-l!" Fran exclaimed, sighing. "Hello there…"

And the Toad Man grinned. "Hello," he said. "You no sink."

"You—you speak our language?" Fran exclaimed rather foolishly.

Toad Man's grin broadened. "Me priest man," he explained proudly. "Me say god-man talk. Make god-man god, no talk. Me talk for god."

"Oh—you mean Thompson," Fran remarked pensively.

"Thomson," the Toad Man agreed. "Good god-man. Show people how make hum-boxes work."

Fran paddled up to the shallow water before him, touched bottom, and stood hip-deep in the water, arms akimbo, her hands on her slim thighs. "What's a hum-box?" she asked brightly.

"Hum-box make hum," explained the Toad Man. "Make cold. Make hot. Cook for meat, no fire."

"A stove?"

The Toad Man blinked owlishly, then shrugged. "Low fella got hum-box," he said. "More better than fire. Low fella you, more white. People go for hum-box. Low fella kill."

Fran grimaced with horror. "You went down there just to get stoves—electric plates—and they shot you!" she exclaimed timorously. "Like—like you were animals..."

"Low fella stick make light," the Toad Man said flatly. "Light make boom. People dead."

"You poor thing," Fran murmured in a soft, hurt tone. And with that, she waded right out of the pool, sat down beside the Toad Man, and put a comforting arm around his shoulders. "You poor thing—"

And then, quite unexpectedly, the Toad Man puckered his broad lips, turned, and gave her a resounding kiss.

Fran stumbled backward and sat down, hard. *"Well!"* she exclaimed.

It was then that Kim's uncontrolled laughter came braying from the brush across the pool.

The Toad Man stiffened instantly, whirled, and grabbed up his spear.

Then he was a quick blur of movement vanishing up the rocky wall. He was gone in seconds.

Samson rose to his feet, rifle cradled on his arm. "They sure do move fast," he remarked thoughtfully.

Kim rolled down out of the brush and sat on the other side of the pool, holding his sides and laughing. He stared across at Fran, stammering with mirth, "Th—the *expression on your f—face!*"

Then he roared with laughter.

Fran got up and brushed the sand off her wet bottom with a grim deliberation. She had been on a frontier world for quite some time, now, and had learned words that hadn't been heard on Earth for decades. Firmly and heatedly, she began to use them.

She used all of them, with sharp effectiveness. Kim and Samson listened with a frank, open-mouthed admiration.

When she had finally exhausted her newfound vocabulary, she marched around the pool and began struggling wetly into her brown coverall.

Kim asked, in a cautious murmur, "Where's your helmet?"

"Didn't wear one!" she snapped back. Then, with a hard tug on her coverall zipper, she explained, "Dimitrios thought the air up here might be breathable. Thompson said he lived up here without a filter-helmet, remember? So they made some tests. Dimitrios says that the poisonous gasses are either so hot they stay up in the cloud-blanket or are so heavy they sink down to the Low Swamps. It's breathable, up here, because the mountains shelter these valleys."

"Speaking of Dimitrios," Samson reminded, "we'd better get moving. Those Gep Tzong won't take forever to come storming back this way."

"If you two hadn't homed in," Fran flared angrily, "I'd have made *friends* with him."

"You certainly would," Kim taunted mildly. "But we aren't talking about that one, Fran." He stood up and slung his rifle over his shoulder. "Samson's right," he added. Let's get moving."

CHAPTER TEN
Attack!

THEY squatted on the hard packed ground beside Dimitrios' cat, while their *ghrakko* dogs drowsed in the shadow of the nearby trees, and Kim, Throwback and Fran made their reports.

Dimitrios nodded grimly. "We've got four people down with fungus fever, too," he told them. "Maybe this fresh, breathable air up here will help them." None of them wore their helmets, nor did anyone in the bustling camp around them.

Kim puffed on a cigarette and drew lines in the dirt with his forefinger. "The MacSneary bunch is here," he said. "The Gep Tzong are here. We're in the middle. The Gep Tzong are mad at the MacSneary bunch."

"Q.e.d., we've got to get *out* of the middle," Samson quipped wryly. "There's another valley up above here. We go up this valley and over a pass between two chimney-peaks. I'll scout ahead."

"And I want four good men on our other *ghrakko* mounts with me," Kim said. "We've got to cover our tracks, and it'll be plenty of work."

Dimitrios nodded again.

They moved. That night, Kim led his weary riders into the new camp in the next valley. Fran brought him his dinner and stood beside him as he wolfed it down. Then he crawled into their cat, mumbled "hello" to Winnetka Jones, and fell into his bunk.

Fran shook him awake in the darkness. "Samson's outside," she whispered. "He wants to see you."

Kim crawled out of his bunk and eased his tired, worn body down from the cat. A small campfire sputtered in the cool early morning darkness, with people clustered silently around it. Kim strode over and clapped Samson on the shoulder. "What's up?"

Samson peered around at him. Kim started. The handsome, black features were almost gray with pallor.

"They moved through the valley behind us!" the tall scout exclaimed huskily. "Over three thousand of 'em, Kim. They marched right through like a well-trained army, just before nightfall!"

"Did they spot our tracks?"

Samson shook his head. "I couldn't tell," he whispered. The whites of his eyes showed plainly in the darkness. "Lordy! Three thousand against sixty, Kim! In this pitch-black Venus night—"

Kim reached out and gripped the big man's arm, tightly. "I'll go with you," he said. "We'll follow them and see what happened. We'll find out which way the Gep Tzong are coming back—"

Fran brought a saddled *ghrakko* dog for him. Then, when it kneeled down, she had to boost him into the saddle. She didn't say a word, but simply kissed him, quickly, before the dog scrambled to its feet. Dimitrios came up with saddlebags of food and canteens of water. Then they were off, loping through the dark night. The rolling, jarring stride of the dogs soon jolted Kim into complete wakefulness.

They found MacSneary's cats at noon. The cats were parked in a night-camp circle in the middle of a small blue-grass valley.

"Lordy…" Samson muttered. "Came down out o' the night and crawled right into their cats with 'em. Sentries posted on watch must've been cut down without a sound."

One of the cats' turbines was rumbling softly. Kim dismounted and climbed inside, ignoring the limp corpses sprawled grotesquely on their bunks. A few minutes later, the turbine stopped. He climbed down and began following a thin, black power-cable off into a clump of trees nearby. Samson followed him, leading the dogs.

The dogs began to snort and paw at the ground before they reached the trees. Then a variant breeze brought them the smell.

Kim stood silently at the edge of the trees, gazing in among them. "They learned how to rig an electric heating-coil, too," he remarked hoarsely.

There was a large, bald head with a luxurious black beard. There were three other heads—a blonde, a brunette, and a redhead. They protruded from the ground like ripe, red melons with hair. They were close together, in a bunch, where the four bodies had been buried to the neck in a hole, with a heating-coil wound around them and the dirt packed in solidly. They were thoroughly roasted.

IT was late night when the two scouts rode back into their own camp. They almost fell from the saddles of the kneeling dogs. Firm, gentle hands helped them over to the campfire and handed them steaming plates of food and mugs of coffee.

"The tracks don't turn back," Kim croaked wearily. "We followed them long enough to make sure. The Gep Tzong have gone on down to the High Slopes—to the swamp plantations—"

"You mean," Dimitrios asked, "they passed up the MacSneary columns?"

"MacSneary's dead," Samson replied curtly. "They're all dead."

By morning, the convoy was on the move again. Kim slept the deep sleep of exhaustion in his bunk, oblivious of the lurching, jolting ride.

When he finally awakened, it was nightfall again and the cats were parked in a camp.

The first thing he noticed as he climbed down from the cat was that all their cats weren't there. He paused, counting the big vehicles in the circle. There were twenty. Five were missing.

Fran came running from the crowd gathered about the campfire. She grabbed him and kissed him. "Samson's over at the fire. He's in charge now," she explained breathlessly.

Kim strode over and looked around the circle of faces at the fire. "Five cats are gone," he said gruffly. "And Dimitrios. Why?"

"They went ahead," Samson spoke from across the fire. "With the Gep Tzong on the warpath, Dimitrios didn't want to risk all of us. He's gone on with five cats to see if he can find the Gep Tzong village before their main body gets back."

"And if he doesn't come back, we return to Venusport?"

Samson nodded silently.

Fran nudged Kim, handed him a steaming plate and mug. Kim squatted beside the fire and gulped the food down, hungrily.

Dimitrios, he concluded, had gone ahead with as few scientific members of the expedition as he'd thought he needed. Kim and Samson were left behind with the rest to guide them back to Venusport—and to see that they got there. It was a sound strategic move.

Then, over coffee and cigarette, Kim remembered something else. "Radio can't reach over these mountains," he said pensively. "How do we keep in contact?"

Samson grinned in defeat. "Dimitrios took all our mounts but one," he said. "He'll send riders back to report, regularly." Then he sobered, knowing what Kim's next question would be.

"When was the first rider due back?"

"At nightfall. He isn't here yet."

Kim scowled darkly. "If he isn't here by morning, I'm riding after them."

The rider didn't appear, so midmorning found Kim riding up the steep trail that skirted the ridge of a gigantic chimney-peak. The tracks of the five cats were easy to follow, but the *ghrakko* dog snorted and trembled beneath him, and climbed wearily, with long, wheezing breaths.

They reached a narrow valley that was perched on the sheer flank of the peak, like an immense ledge. Torn wisps of crimson fog lay close to the ground. Above, the orange-red cloud-blanket glowered like the landscape of Hell turned upside down. The valley-on-a-ledge curved around to where the peak's flank joined a neighboring peak, and there was a deep, narrow gap through the rock. There were other tracks beside the cat-tread tracks, too. Thousands of web-footed tracks.

Kim was thrown clear when the *ghrakko* dog collapsed. It rolled over, breathing with great, wheezing gasps. Kim climbed to his feet, pulled his rifle out of the sand, and put the dog out of its misery with a well-aimed shot. Then he trudged onward, afoot.

He rounded a bend in the narrow gap and almost stumbled into the rear cat in the column. A cat-driver glanced back, then raised a shout. Dimitrios came running from the head of the column.

"Kim!" he exclaimed. "I might've known you'd show up."

"Why aren't you farther ahead?" Kim retorted. "I didn't expect to catch up with you before night."

The scientist trotted up, stopped, and shook his head. "Had to go slow," he gasped. "Our dogs couldn't take it. Want to keep 'em, if we can. Where's yours?"

"Keeled over, back there." Kim grimaced. "What's holding you up, now?"

Dimitrios gestured toward the front of the column. "Come up here and I'll show you."

Kim followed him up to the first cat and stared as Dimitrios stopped and pointed ahead.

On the sandy floor between the sheer walls of the gap stood a large brazier of hammered bronze. Coals flamed white-hot in its open pan. A dense cloud of oily blue smoke boiled up from it, completely obscuring the end of the gap.

It stood about four hundred yards ahead of the cats.

"We reached here less than an hour ago," Dimitrios commented in hushed tones. "We've been waiting for it to burn out, but it hasn't. I think someone's feeding it fresh coals from the other side."

"In that case," Kim replied, "the only thing to do is go down and look." He checked the settings on his Chavez rifle and sauntered ahead, toward the smoke-spewing brazier.

"Careful!" Dimitrios called after him. "We'll cover you. If you see anything—get back here."

"Uh huh," Kim grunted. He strode onward.

THERE wasn't a sound, save his boots crunching in the coarse sand. As he approached the brazier, he noted that it was as tall as he was, shaped like a huge, bronze urn. Its sides were inscribed with weird etchings.

The walls rose sheer and blank on either side. Ahead, there was only the brazier and its dense cloud of blue smoke billowing upward.

Then he heard it. Far off, somewhere. A faint rumbling sound, like thunder. He froze in his tracks, instantly.

Then the rumbling grew to a vast roar that shook the ground beneath him, that jerked him around to gaze upward in horror.

High on the walls of the gap, hundreds of feet above the cats, great masses of rock were breaking loose, crumbling, hurtling downward. Kim waved his arms and shouted frantically, but his shouts were lost in the tremendous roar. He could see Dimitrios standing before the lead cat, staring at him in puzzlement. The scientist's brown figure stood out sharply against the cat's blunt, blackened prow...

Then a vast cloud of swirling dust enveloped him. Swallowed him, the cats, the whole end of the gap. There was a mighty blast of sound and concussion that threw Kim to his knees.

The dust billowed up gently, revealing vague glimpses of the great pile of jagged, broken rock that completely filled the gap.

Kim stumbled to his feet with a sob.

A shrill, shrieking cry swung him back toward the huge brazier. He stood swaying, staring drunkenly, as a withering mass of greenish-gray toadish forms came quickly around the bronze urn, running straight toward him.

The Chavez seemed to come up in his hands of its own accord. Its dazzling bolts licked out, struck the onrushing mass, blasted great gaps in their ranks, and exploded torn, mangled bodies against the sheer walls. But they came on.

Kim threw down the Chavez in disgust and whipped out his Maxims. The beams lanced out from his fists, ripped open bulbous, pale chests. Toad-like bodies began to pile up before him. They piled four-deep right up to his boots. Then the toad hordes from behind them came swarming over, slamming into him, throwing him back onto the sand. Hard fists pummeled him, crashed against his head, beat him senseless. The squirming greenish-gray mass became a roaring blackness...

ONE thing had impressed him. As he had blown the many toad shapes apart, their flesh and blood had been revealed as a bright, wet scarlet. Like human blood. And they were mammals.

He lay there, thinking about that for awhile. Until he realized that he had regained consciousness.

He was staring up at a ceiling of straight, slender poles chinked with mud. It was the ceiling of a small, low room, and the walls were of some woven matting.

A sharp twinge of pain lanced through his skull as he raised his head. He saw that he was sprawled on a low pallet of furry skins and there was an odd toad-like female squatting just inside the narrow doorway. Then dizziness overcame him and he slumped back with a groan.

A tremendous, throbbing ache seemed to permeate his whole body. He lay in a daze, hardly aware of his surroundings.

A short while later—it may have been hours—he felt something being forced between his lips. Cool, refreshing liquid spilled into his throat. He swallowed painfully.

Later, he slept.

The odd, half-naked woman seemed never to leave the room. As Kim's strength came back, he began to notice that daylight and darkness passed outside the doorway, and he guessed that he was in a small hut. The Gep Tzong woman cooked his meals on a small brazier, fed him, and packed hot, foul-smelling black mud on the livid cuts and bruises on his body. She cleaned the hut every morning. She slept while squatting beside the doorway, leaning back against the wall. She made a few efforts at speech, at first, in a harsh, guttural language; then she lapsed into silence.

Kim felt the strength flowing back into his limbs as the pain left him. His bruises vanished, and the woman packed mud onto fewer and fewer cuts.

But he never attempted to stir from his pallet. He never spoke once. Only when the woman's back was turned would he move his arms and legs, flexing and massaging his sore muscles.

He listened attentively to the sounds outside the hut. Footsteps padding past, guttural voices. Firelight flickered through the doorway at night, and then there was the monotonous, booming thunder of the drums. Every night, they lulled him to sleep.

Finally, he had a visitor. A Gep Tzong man stepped into the hut one morning and dismissed the woman with a jerk of his head. He came over and stood above Kim, staring down at him.

"God-man no speak!" he intoned harshly.

Kim lay motionless, making no reply.

The Toad Man grinned broadly. "God-man speak! Me hear speak!" he exclaimed happily. "God-man play no speak. Play sick!"

Still, Kim didn't utter a sound.

The Toad Man whirled and stalked out. The woman slipped back into the hut, instantly.

That night, the guttural voices were louder. And the drums boomed faster. Kim lay on his pallet, staring out at the darkness, watching the firelight reflection leap and dance on the hut's dirt floor. He licked his lips, nervously, shot repeated glances at the woman. But she merely squatted by the door, seeming to doze.

Then they came for him.

Glistening, greenish bodies coming through the doorway, bony hands grasping him, roughly, bearing him from the pallet. They half-dragged, half-carried him from the hut. And the drums increased their pace to an insane, booming thunder.

Then they released him, left him standing weakly. And there was silence. Tense, heavy silence.

He was standing before a broad clearing. Meat roasted on the spits over a great fire blazing at the far end of the clearing. Between him and the fire, naked, toad people sat in two long rows, facing each other. Between the rows were heaped baskets of fruit, jugs, vases, bowls, and platters of steaming food. Their heads were all turned toward him, staring at him with their large, liquid eyes.

Staring through him, beyond him. At something behind him.

Slowly, Kim turned.

Behind him was a high stone dais. Mounted on the dais was a stout wooden pillory. There were leather straps on the pillory to bind a man's hands and arms. And between them were other straps, fashioned like a muzzle for an animal. A muzzle that would hold a man's head still and bind his jaws wide open so they could reach in and grasp his tongue.

Kim moved with blinding speed, snatched a barbed spear from the nearest warrior, and charged through them. Instantly the mass of toad bodies surged over him, bearing him to the ground. Voices raised in guttural shrieks and the drums boomed triumphantly. They lifted him to their shoulders, carried him up on the dais, and bound his arms to the pillory.

Then they stepped back, grinning. They hadn't bound the muzzle over his head. They waited for him to speak. To scream.

CHAPTER ELEVEN
Temple of the Toad Men

As the darkness faded to the deep purple gloom of morning, Kim saw the village. It was a wild cluster of thousands of mud-roofed huts beyond the clearing.

His wrists stung with pain. His arms ached numbly. Blood clotted the straps binding them. He had long since stopped straining, giving it up with exhausted resignation. As the purple twilight gathered, he was ready to become their god.

The fire had died to glowing embers on the far side of the clearing. The air was cool and still. The long night was past. Guttural voices had chanted, drums had boomed, and the Gep Tzong had feasted well. Hundreds of them were sprawled out in the clearing, snoring with a drunken, well-fed contentment.

It had been a ceremonial feast in their god-man's honor. When they awakened, Kim knew, the ceremony would resume. There was a small brazier glowing on the stone dais before him. A large, wooden pincers lay beside the brazier. And in the smoldering coals lay a thin, sharp dagger, its blade glowing white-hot.

He could look at it almost without shuddering now. The pain wouldn't be too bad, he reasoned; it wouldn't last more than a few days. Then he would be their god! Maybe he could do something for them, something that would end this era of horror.

The sky deepened to a dark, smoky violet and he could see beyond the village. He could see the dark forests cloaking the slopes of their valley and the dim, naked walls of the mountains that hemmed it.

And then he could see their temple. He was sure it was that. It stood up against the foot of a steep cliff rising behind their village. It was a tall tower, jet-black, pointing upward several hundred feet to a sharp, tapered point. A stone stairway cut into the face of the cliff extended upward to a round, dark opening in the side of the tower.

This was the temple of the sacred metal. The temple where their gods went to die.

Kim stared at the sleeping greenish-gray figures—waiting. It would be over quickly enough, he thought. It wouldn't take long. And then...

He felt a cold, icy touch against his right arm. He turned his head and stared, wide-eyed. A curved, steel blade was sawing carefully through the leather straps. Kim uttered a choking, strangled gasp.

"Quiet, darling," a voice whispered behind him.

He clamped his mouth shut to keep from shouting. He trembled violently.

The straps fell away and his numbed arms flopped at his sides. Then Fran's slender, soft figure slipped around the pillory and caught him before he fell. She gave a faint, whimpering sob as he leaned heavily against her. She helped him down from the dais and across the clearing into the trees.

"Please, Kim," she murmured beseechingly. "You've got to walk. I can't carry you, darling."

Kim felt a sudden, blazing anger surge up through him. He straightened up, his mouth twisting with hatred, and swung back toward the clearing. Fran grabbed him, clung to him. "Kim, no! We've got to get away! Kim—"

"Not—yet!" His voice grated in his throat. He pulled her arms from his neck, pushed her aside. As she stumbled back, he saw that Maxim pistols were belted to her thighs. A Chavez was slung over her shoulder and a small knapsack was strapped to her back.

He reached out and pulled the Chavez from her shoulder, checked its settings, and slung it over his own.

"Temple," he said thickly. "Treasure—we get that!"

The anger burning inside him like a consuming flame, he turned and led the way, stumbling and weaving, up through the trees. Around the sprawling village. Toward the stairway hewn into the steep cliff face.

Fran grabbed his arm when they reached the foot of the stairs. "No, Kim! You'll kill yourself. The radioactivity—"

Kim snorted in disgust and pointed upward to where a twisting green vine coiled around the black tower and writhed into its round opening. "That lives!" he croaked raspingly.

Fran released him and stepped back, gazing up at him, bleakly. Her hand dipped down and pulled out one of the Maxim pistols. "I'll wait," she said dully.

Kim climbed the stone stairway. He reached the round opening in the tower and stopped. The tower was constructed of some solid, black mold that was flaked and crumbling. He moved toward it, hesitantly, stepped through the round opening. The mold crunched beneath his feet.

He stood within a small, circular chamber. A round hole in the rough, flaking black ceiling led upward to another chamber. But there was no opening into the lower part of the tower—the larger part. He walked under the ceiling hole, reached up, and hauled himself through it.

Another circular chamber, with light filtering in through a jagged crack in the black wall. And another opening, leading upward. He hauled himself through it.

The last chamber was small, cramped. With crumbling, black mounds against the walls. He stared at them, dumbly.

Then he walked over and kicked at one. It collapsed in a pile of black, rotted flakes. He kicked another. It collapsed. And tiny yellow flakes spilled out with the black. Crumbling, yellow flakes and—something else. Something square, bright, silvery, that came sliding to the crusted floor.

Kim stared down at it. Then, slowly, he stooped and picked it up.

He lowered himself back down to the bottom chamber, stepped out through the round opening, and strode quickly down the stone stairway. He stopped at the bottom, turned, and stared back up at the tall, black tower.

"What is it, Kim?" Fran asked faintly.

He held the silvery object out for her to see...

THEY walked out of the Misty Mountains. They found the three abandoned cats in the valley. Fran told how the returning war party had attacked them, how they blazed their way through with flame-jelly, and how the last three cats had been cut off. They found Throwback Samson standing before a nearby tree, an expression of stunned surprise on his face. The shaft of a spear protruded from his chest, pinning him solidly to the tree.

They gathered supplies from the abandoned cats, donned filter-helmets, and went on.

CHAPTER TWELVE
The Conquest of Venus

SUMMER on Venus was the season when the rains reversed. In winter, it poured out of the clouds. In summer, it steamed out of the mud. On Venus, in summertime, it was seldom that a man could see five feet ahead of him through the dense, hot mists.

Summer passed, and the clear, autumnal season came, when the orange-red clouds blazed high above and the beautiful, terrifying landscape below stood out sharply, sparkling clear. The trail twisted down from the volcanic hill, through the blue fronds, and up onto the flat, rocky plain where the huge dome of Venusport stood gleaming.

The two *ghrakko* dogs mounted the trail with a slow, weary plodding and halted gratefully as their riders drew rein at the edge of the plain. The man and woman gazed longingly at the giant metal dome of the city, with its myriad glints of glassite ports. Neither of them spoke.

Then they prodded their mounts on up the muddy track, into the outskirts of the sprawling settlement. They rode slowly, side by side, pistols on their hips and Chavez rifles across their laps. The man was roughly bearded, lean and muscular. The woman's light brown hair was tied in rolls on her neck, compressed within her helmet. The man wore a scant loin-string and the woman a short skirt and bra, cut from the same mottled blue-gray *ghrakko* skin.

Tall, rugged plantation men and hunters stepped aside for them in the crowded, muddy street. Shop proprietors standing outside the domed prefab huts nodded their heads in silent greeting. Groups of rough, heavily armed men standing at the corners stilled their harsh, profane talk as the riders went past.

Such was the custom of the frontier, in deference to Fran, whose matching skin garments proclaimed her to be the woman of the man at her side. Such deference was her due, since a bride on the frontier is more than a mere bride, more than a married woman. She is a definite mother of children, a potential power of life to the community, an embodiment of sheer survival that all must respect.

And Fran was pregnant.

Kim scowled grimly as he surveyed the groups of men and women on the street. The tight gatherings on the corners, the prominence of guns among them-townspeople as well as swamp-men-were features that made him feel tense inside. His hard gaze softened momentarily as he glanced at Fran.

"Too many guns," he commented brusquely. "Somebody's been making history…"

Fran gave a faint frown. "There's no sound of fighting…"

"Uh huh. That means the revolt is over." Kim shook his head, uneasily. "Something else is stirring—which means conditions have changed. And they've maybe changed in a way that's bad for us…"

Fran's smile was gentle, reminiscent. "You worry too much," she remonstrated softly.

Kim gave an unintelligible grunt and shifted the rifle across his lap. "We'd best ride on to the spaceport field," he decided. "Got to have Repair cut that steel beam off the *Voodoo's* locks and get you settled inside and—"

"Call Medical," Fran interjected musingly. "Which is why I'm doubly glad we're here, finally. And lock you up in the control pit so I won't have to worry about you going out and getting into trouble."

"Got to sell these *ghrakkos*," Kim protested matter-of-factly, "and we'd best check in with the Governor so Earth will be notified you got back safely. Then you won't need a lock to keep me on the *Voodoo*—" His voice grew husky with emotion.

Fran reached across and laid a comforting hand on his arm. "Poor man," she murmured.

THERE were six giant Space Fleet dreadnoughts on the field, instead of two. The field was crawling with blue-uniformed troops. Kim led the way through the tangle of other spacecraft, heaving an explosive sigh of relief when he spotted the *Voodoo*, still squatting where he had left it.

An hour later, with Fran comfortably established in the little ship's stateroom and a Medical physician in attendance, Kim rode his dog and led the other back to the outskirts of town where he found a pole corral and a *ghrakko* dealer's hut. There followed another hour of haggling while he squeezed a fair price out of the shrewd dealer. Then he was strolling up to the giant airlocks and entering the vast, bustling dome of Venusport. He was one of many men of Venus, as he strode along the busy corridors, pistols on his thighs and a tanned-hide kitbag swinging at his side.

The anteroom to the Governor's office was filled with smooth-cheeked, young, blue-uniformed Fleet officers who were carrying on a mild flirtation with the pert, blonde receptionist at the desk. The receptionist ignored five handsome, attentive officers long enough to tell Kim that Governor Serkov was in conference and couldn't be disturbed.

"Tell him Kim Rothman is here," Kim said flatly, "and he'll be plenty disturbed."

The blonde arched her delicate eyebrows, dubiously, but she put through the call. A voice snapped from her desk intercom screen. She looked rather startled as she faced Kim, again. "Please wait, Mr. Rothman. Commander Kruger will see you in a few minutes."

Kim nodded curtly and strolled over to a comfortable chair near the wall.

He had no sooner seated himself than a tall, thin Fleet officer came striding over, hand outstretched. "Kim!" he exclaimed joyfully.

Kim stared up at the thin, pointed, walnut-brown face. Then he was on his feet, pumping the officer's hand. "Korsak!" he blurted, his gaze running down the trim, blue uniform. "Korsak—not you!"

The tall Mars colonist laughed heartily. "Quite a change, isn't it?" Other Fleet officers were gathering around, grinning.

"Change!" Kim gasped. "Why, the last time I saw you, you were leading a pirate party out in spacesuits to board a crippled freighter—"

"shhhh!" Korsak silenced mockingly. "Not so loud. I'm a respectable officer of the Space Fleet, now, or I might mention who was piloting that pirate craft."

"But—" Kim eased himself cautiously back into his chair, still staring. "But how in blazes did you ever come to *this?*"

Korsak shook his head in mock sadness. "Ah, Kim, old friend, the Universe has come to a strange path. The whole Solar System is aflame with violent deeds. Revolution on Venus, then that crowd of dirty scum that moved out on the Ring. D'you know there are pirates raiding shipments to the free settlements of Mars and Venus, now, and taking their loot to the corporation holders in the Jovian System?"

Kim's eyes narrowed in recollection. "So that's it, eh? A gang tried to get me in on that deal before I left Ceresport."

"That," Korsak said emphatically, "is the deal. And they've got the worst scum in the System doing their dirty work. Take women prisoners and murder the men—"

"So you joined the Space Fleet?"

"I was—ahem—offered a commission," Korsak explained apologetically. "Seems these Space Fleet rookies never could catch anything in these big, lumbering dreadnoughts, so they've acquired the habit of commissioning us privateers in our small craft to go after the scum. They pay good, too. You ought to look into—"

"Excuse me..." The blonde receptionist was at Korsak's elbow. She spoke to Kim. "Commander Kruger will see you, now. In his office."

Kim rose and followed her to the inner doorway.

"Keep it in mind," Korsak called after him. Kim nodded absently and strolled on.

THERE were the twin, blue-uniformed guards, the tall ivory portals that swung sedately open. And the beefy, powerful visage of Commander Kruger, behind the desk. At the side of the desk sat a girl, a secretary, with notepad and stylus.

"Sit down, Mr. Rothman," Kruger spoke cordially. "Congratulations on your return. We thought you were dead. The others arrived eight months ago and have already returned to Earth."

"Mrs. Rothman has also returned," Kim said, stepping forward and sprawling into a chair.

"Mrs. Rothman?"

"Miss Frances Freemont," Kim explained.

Kruger nodded. "I see. All right, Mr. Rothman. I want to hear your report. Tell me everything that happened."

Kim settled back, puffed a cigarette alight, and launched into his narrative. Kruger's secretary took it down.

"—And so," Kim concluded, "Fran left the remaining seventeen cats and came back after me. She got me out of the Gep Tzong village just in time to save me from becoming a god."

Hmmm..." Kruger pursed his lips, thoughtfully. "So you were actually in the Gep Tzong village?"

"That's right."

"Most interesting..." Kruger rose with sudden decision. "Wait here a moment, Mr. Rothman." He hurried out, leaving Kim and a thoroughly awed young secretary.

But it was only a moment before he came bustling back, and motioned Kim to follow him.

They went down a deep-carpeted corridor and entered another tall ivory doorway. Kim paused uncertainly as they walked into a wide, low-ceilinged chamber. There was a long conference table in the center of the room; Governor Serkov sat at the head of the table. With him were a half-dozen high-ranking Space Fleet officers.

"Mr. Rothman," said Serkov, "sit down..."

Kim walked to the foot of the table and dropped into a chair.

"You say you were in the Gep Tzong village?"

Kim nodded.

"Tell us everything you can about them," one of the blue-uniformed officers demanded somewhat curtly. "Give us every single detail you recall..."

Kim stared at him. "Why?"

The officer's face reddened. There was a general stir of movement around the table.

"Mr. Rothman," Governor Serkov spoke gravely, "the situation has altered considerably since you were last in

Venusport. Part of that alteration, you must perceive, was caused by the expedition of which you were a member—"

"No..." Kim shook his head. "I don't perceive anything. Suppose you explain it to me?"

Serkov's lips twitched impatiently. "Thanks to the efforts of that expedition to 'pacify' the Gep Tzong savages, the settlers of Venus were subjected to a severe raid in which hundreds were killed and nearly a thousand wounded."

"I wasn't aware of that fact," Kim said soberly.

"You are now. So suppose you answer some questions?"

"Gladly."

"What sort of intelligence would you credit the Gep Tzong as having?"

"A very cunning intelligence."

" As high as ours?"

"Definitely. A bit more savage, in a very human way—"

"How well-organized are these savages?"

"Very well organized in a militant religious society. Their tribal armies are undoubtedly under religious leadership."

A Fleet officer sighed resignedly. "Savages. Fanatical barbarism. They won't be easy to whip..."

"Do you intend to whip them?" Kim asked coldly.

"No question about it," the officer retorted. "You can make some sort of deal with savages only if those savages respect you. These Gep Tzong have raided and pillaged and escaped unchallenged; they'll not respect us for that."

Another official cleared his throat, then added: "That's the situation in a nutshell. We'll have to march out and teach these devils a lesson. Then—and only then—will we be able to make a deal with them."

And a third officer spoke up: "But that's savagery, itself. I can't see civilized men stooping that low—"

"Then keep your eyes closed," the second snapped. "We're dealing with savages, and savages respect only certain things. You have to deal with 'em in their own way, or not at all."

"And," the first chimed in, "we've *got* to deal with them. We need Venus. We need those mountain regions, where the atmosphere's clear and breathable—"

"But Venus belongs to *them*," the third argued. "What right have we to come in and start pushing them around?"

"No right whatever," Kim snapped suddenly. "Unfortunately, however, the pushing has already been done. I'm afraid you men are right—you'll have to give them a licking before they'll respect you again."

"Thank you, Mr. Rothman," Serkov spoke sarcastically. "I am sure we all appreciate hearing you admit your expedition was the cause of this."

"I think what Mr. Rothman refers to," countered the second officer, "is the merciless way Venus settlers were killing the Gep Tzong, as though they were beasts. I understand that was your personal opinion of them, too, Governor Serkov."

Serkov's face turned gray. He opened his mouth to speak, but the first officer beat him to it.

"The fact remains," this erstwhile, silver-haired man said, "that Venus is not and never was an open planet just ripe for human settlement. What's happened has happened—we can't change it now—and we were all at least partly to blame for it."

"Oh, were we?" Serkov snorted disdainfully. "And what about these fools who were after that so-called 'sacred metal' of the Gep Tzong—"

"It's still there," Kim interrupted quietly.

"What?"

"And it could still be made lethally radioactive, I suppose, if you had the mechanisms necessary to handle it," he added. Slowly, he rose to his feet and faced them down the long table. "Gentlemen, your debate has been most interesting. However, there are a few things I would like to add—

"First, the Gep Tzong are not some species of wild animal. The settlers of Venus know that, now. They've learned it the hard way. And they are going to learn, further, that the Gep Tzong is no mere form of savagely intelligent monster they can do away with easily, without qualms. *The Gep Tzong are not alien.*

"You've depicted the Gep Tzong as some life-form of relatively low intelligence which has evolved on Venus but hasn't been capable of building itself any recognizable form of civilization above the lowest stage of barbarism. In a way, you may be right; but as facts go, gentlemen, you're wrong.

"The Gep Tzong have a legend that claims they're descendants of gods who came down from the mountaintops. These gods built a black temple and gave birth to the first generation of Gep Tzong. The temple is there; I've been inside it. But shortly after the first generation was born—the Adams and Eves of the Gep Tzong—their gods died, all but one.

"Maybe those gods died from radioactive burns, but I doubt it—burns also kill sperm. More likely, they died because they fell down in the Misty Mountains and weren't inoculated against the diseases of Venus. And the sole survivor who became the teacher of the first Gep Tzong generation was unable to talk. He was a mute! And that's not an uncommon result of severe shock.

"No, gentlemen, you're dead wrong about the Gep Tzong. They're different—they're greenish and toad-like. Maybe that's the effect of the Venusian atmosphere. Maybe it didn't come with one generation, but developed gradually through a hundred and seventy years of inbreeding. I don't know. My—my wife doesn't know—

"But the Gep Tzong are not alien. And furthermore, I can prove it…" He jerked the kitbag from his side and tugged at its thongs. It came open and his hand dipped inside. "I found this in their temple," he finished gravely. "It is the true account of the gods of the Gep Tzong—"

With that, he pulled his hand out and tossed the square, silvery object on the table before them. It clattered loudly on the glossy surface.

They sat staring at it, speechlessly. At the heavy permalloy cover, the thin permalloy sheets. Made to last for eons, to withstand the worst of conditions.

Across its stained, warped silver face was the deeply etched inscription:

LOG OF THE
S. S. STARLING III

Tall ivory portals swung silently open. The blonde receptionist appeared, stared uncertainly at the stiff statues around the table, then beckoned to Kim. "Audiovisor call for you, Mr. Rothman. From the spaceport field." She turned and hurried over to a wall screen. "You can take it here."

Kim strode over to the screen, quickly. The girl tuned the studs expertly, then stepped aside.

Fran's round, full face gazed out at him. Her eyelids drooped sleepily. "Kim—" she murmured softly. "Kim. They say—it's almost time—" Then, abruptly, the screen went blank.

Kim whirled and marched to the doorway. He paused there, between the tall ivory portals, and looked back at the men seated around the table.

"Gentlemen," he said gruffly, "I leave you an open planet. Good luck to you."

Then, he was gone.

THE END

ARMCHAIR SCI-FI, FANTASY, & HORROR DOUBLE NOVELS, $12.95 each

D-81   **THE LAST PLEA** by Robert Bloch
THE STATUS CIVILIZATION by Robert Sheckley

D-82   **WOMAN FROM ANOTHER PLANET** by Frank Belknap Long
HOMECALLING by Judith Merril

D-83   **WHEN TWO WORLDS MEET** by Robert Moore Williams
THE MAN WHO HAD NO BRAINS by Jeff Sutton

D-84   **THE SPECTRE OF SUICIDE SWAMP** by E. K. Jarvis
IT'S MAGIC, YOU DOPE! by Jack Sharkey

D-85   **THE STARSHIP FROM SIRIUS** by Rog Phillips
THE FINAL WEAPON by Everett Cole

D-86   **TREASURE ON THUNDER MOON** by Edmond Hamilton
TRAIL OF THE ASTROGAR by Henry Haase

D-87   **THE VENUS ENIGMA** by Joe Gibson
THE WOMAN IN SKIN 13 by Paul W. Fairman

D-88   **THE MAD ROBOT** by William P. McGivern
THE RUNNING MAN by J. Holly Hunter

D-89   **VENGEANCE OF KYVOR** by Randall Garrett
AT THE EARTH'S CORE by Edgar Rice Burroughs

D-90   **DWELLERS OF THE DEEP** by Don Wilcox
NIGHT OF THE LONG KNIVES by Fritz Leiber

ARMCHAIR SCIENCE FICTION CLASSICS, $12.95 each

C-28   **THE MAN FROM TOMORROW**
by Stanton A. Coblentz

C-29   **THE GREEN MAN OF GRAYPEC**
by Festus Pragnell

C-30   **THE SHAVER MYSTERY, Book Four**
by Richard S. Shaver

ARMCHAIR MASTERS OF SCIENCE FICTION SERIES, $16.95 each

MS-7   **MASTERS OF SCIENCE FICTION AND FANTASY, Vol. Seven**
Lester Del Rey, "The Band Played On" and other tales

MS-8   **MASTERS OF SCIENCE FICTION, Vol. Eight**
Milton Lesser, "'A' is for Android" and other tales

TERROR FROM OUT OF THE SKY...

The ship came down into Lake Michigan around four o'clock in the morning, early in the month of June. It came very quietly for so large a ship, and the aliens riding within were amazingly swift and dreadfully efficient. These aliens—the Argans—were humanoid in appearance but the color of their skin was different. Like a quick-moving, deadly plague they moved in on Chicago, taking over the city before anyone really knew what was happening! They were intelligent and ruthless—and their hold over the city seemed impenetrable.

But when a female alien was captured, the government came up with a desperate scheme: send in an Earth woman—her skinned tinted green—to impersonate a female alien and find a weakness to the aliens' hold on the city.

CAST OF CHARACTERS

MARY WINSTON
To do her job in the best Mata Hari tradition would probably incur a "'fate worse than death." But she had a lot of faith in fate.

MARK CLAYTON
He was the head of C4, the top echelon of government Intelligence—and most dependable when things got tough.

GLAN
This alien had no desire to invade the Earth—he only wanted to insure the success of an underground alien resistance.

MARA ZO
An alien—she was captured by Earth's military and her personality transferred to an Earth agent by Professor Halley.

PROFESSOR HALLEY
A brilliant scientist, he designed the "costumes" for the agents to wear when they infiltrated the alien invaders' stronghold.

MORN
Tales were told of this dreaded leader of the Argans—about his savagery in both business and pleasure.

THE
WOMAN IN
SKIN 13

By
PAUL W. FAIRMAN

ARMCHAIR FICTION
PO Box 4369, Medford, Oregon   97501-0168

CHAPTER ONE

THE SHIP came down into Lake Michigan around four o'clock in the morning early in the month of June. It came very quietly for so large a ship, and the people riding it were amazingly swift and dreadfully efficient. Like a deadly plague they moved in on Chicago, and before anyone got around to doing anything about the invasion, it was too late.

They had a vast assortment of weapons. On the basis of results achieved, the Army certified to: (1) a hand weapon, utilizing heat as ammunition, which left little of its target in recognizable condition; (2) a portable ray mechanism which functioned as a hypnotic inducer, turning crowds of angry, bewildered, or hostile people into little better than docile cattle herds; (3) some device for doming over a given area under a thickness of vibration—probably ultrasonic—capable of prematurely exploding any missile known to the Army. This curtain was also lethal.

The invaders obviously moved by a carefully preconceived plan. Their first objective was the complete ejection of native population from a prefixed area—this area being the City of Chicago and suburbs, to a perimeter of farmland, forest, and open country. They were markedly humane during this operation, killing as few of the residents as possible, and showing every consideration so far as was practicable to the aged, babies, mothers, small children, and cripples.

They were chillingly inhuman in their insistence on complete evacuation, even to the sick from the hospitals and the insane from asylums both public and private. They were masters in the art of swift, competent administration, achieving the complete evacuation in less than two days; protecting themselves the while from outside attack, and carrying out every detail of the invasion and ejection with an efficiency beyond belief.

The nation seemed to rally to its own defense with a surprising lack of panic and disruption. This, however, was probably the fault of the invaders themselves, the swift completion of their self-appointed and seemingly impossible task having had a shattering effect upon the mind and morale of the people; thus causing a state of stunned bewilderment that could easily be misinterpreted as quiet courage.

The rallying and the counterattack had little constructive effect, however. It resulted in nothing more than the drawing of a tight military ring around the invaded area.

One got the uneasy impression, however, that the tight circle was allowed to exist only by courtesy of the invaders; that it was tolerated because they did not desire—at least at the time—to expand their holdings.

Their defense perimeter was so solid and impenetrable as to constitute complete isolation of the invaded area. No branch of the American government even pretended to know what was going on inside the perimeter.

The period of invasion, evacuation, attempts and complete failures at counter-invasion, lasted somewhat over two weeks. During the attempted counterassault, the intruders made no hostile gestures other than those of defending themselves. And finally the Army was forced to pause and reconsider—much as a stunned and bloodied man must pause and reconsider after butting his head against a stone wall.

The invaders, according to the refugees and the counterattackers, were of two colors. The males were of a violet hue; the females, all the same shade of green. Physically, both sexes were, according to Earth standards, magnificent specimens. They wore little clothing, but seemed entirely comfortable even in the comparative chill of night and early morning.

That was about all anyone knew of them—or so the general public thought.

MARY WINSTON had been on call for over a week when her phone rang. To a C4 agent, "on call" meant staying home within reach of the telephone, until summoned to headquarters. Mary had spent periods as long as thirty days in this boring state. But under present circumstances, the inactive week had seemed like SIX months.

Her call came at one p.m. on the eighth day. She snatched up the phone and tried to sound impersonal; tried to keep the elation out of her voice.

"This is Mark Clayton," the voice said. "We're ready for you."

"I'll be right down."

"Twenty minutes?"

"Ten."

The answer might have been a chuckle. "Fine. Come straight to my office."

Mary overestimated her own speed by two and a half minutes, but there was no censure from the chief as she entered his office.

Mark Clayton looked young for his job. Head of C4, the top echelon of Government Intelligence, the department always depended on him when the going was toughest.

He put his pipe into an ashtray and said, "Sit down, Mary. I don't think they're quite ready for us yet. We'll use the time for a short preliminary briefing."

Mary Winston had not spoken as yet. She took the chair indicated, crossed her ankles, and waited. Mark Clayton let his eyes travel slowly downward, from her blonde head to the brown-and-white pumps she wore so effectively.

An observer would never have suspected these two had dined and danced together not two weeks before; that Mark had kissed Mary good night and had been kissed in return. The look in his eyes as he surveyed her now was impersonal, calculating, analytical.

He said, "We have a job that fits you to a T. This is a clause-five proposition, though. I wish you'd turn it down."

A clause-five job was one which came under certain of the small type in an agent's commission; a job entailing hazards which an agent was not required to undergo.

"I've never invoked the clause yet, Mr. Clayton," Mary said, "and I never intend to." Mr. Clayton! That wasn't the name she'd used the night she'd kissed him back. But they'd been two other people at the time. Now they were chief and subordinate, and one of the basic requirements of an agent was a sense of proportion.

Mark sighed. "No, you haven't. Nor did I expect you to this time. My statement was just a required formality."

MARY DID not reply. But in her mind there was a certain satisfaction; a knowledge that she affected him more than his casual front indicated.

She remained silent and Mark said, "We've gotten a break in Chicago."

"I'm glad."

"Maybe I'm optimistic in calling it a break. Let's say we've been given a slight advantage that we may be able to turn into a break. It depends on you."

"I'll do my best."

Mark's smile was fleeting, barely perceptible. He said, "It will entail your removing your clothing and going around practically naked."

"If it's necessary, I can do that too," Mary replied evenly.

Mark sat down behind his desk, tipped his eyes to the ceiling, and began talking. "About a week ago, one of the females of the Chicago invaders strayed outside their ray-curtain. Our men captured her. She was brought here. She's in the building now.

"We drugged her and put her under the monitor. In two days we had everything we could get from her—a broad though somewhat sketchy background concerning her race and where she came from."

"Nothing of their plans and objectives?"

Mark frowned. "She didn't know a great deal about that; only that they plan to stay."

"Did you learn anything of their weapons?"

Mark shook his head. "No. She appears to be one of the foot soldiers straight out of the ranks. She knows how to use both their hypno-ray and their heat weapon, but she hasn't got the foggiest notion of what makes either of them tick."

"I take it then that both males and females are active fighters. Are they rated equally?"

Mark smiled. The twinkle in his eyes was almost personal. "It would appear that the female is rated the higher; that is, if we haven't underestimated the girl's ego."

Possibly this was supposed to draw a spark, but it didn't. After a moment, Mark went on: "You probably have a pretty good idea already of what your assignment entails."

"The one I'd naturally assume presents obstacles. You said these people had a definite and unmistakable coloring."

Mark arose from his chair. "Let's go on with the second phase of the briefing."

He led Mary through an inner doorway and down a long corridor. He stopped finally and opened another doorway. They entered a small room in which two other people awaited them.

"You've met Prof Halley," Mark said.

"Of course. How do you do, Professor."

Halley's bright eyes took Mary in with appreciation and complete lack of impersonality. "Hello, darling. Long time no see. Have they picked you for this suicide run?"

Mary smiled. Halley was a fussy little chemist—privileged as all geniuses are privileged—and the people who knew him lost the ability to be offended at his frank eyes and franker speech.

"That's what they tell me," Mary said.

HER EYES moved naturally to the fourth occupant of the room. A girl lying wide-eyed upon a table, covered from the neck down by a white sheet. The sheet outlined a long, symmetrical body with which any Earth girl would have been delighted. Also, the contours of the finely molded face met all Earth standards of feminine beauty.

Only the complexion set this female apart. It was—of a soft apple green. Strangely, it was not repulsive. Rather, the effect was that of an exquisite and beautiful mask over a lovely face. The only unpleasant touch—the only flaw—was in the open, staring eyes—unnatural, vacant. But this did not detract too much from the perfection of the overall picture, because on sensed that the resulting expression *was* unnatural.

Without preamble or ceremony Professor Halley jerked the sheet from the girl's body, revealing uncovered symmetry and the soft, apple-green coloring broken only by two white bandages around the thigh of the left leg.

Professor Halley chuckled in delight. "This one was a lulu. Really a lulu, but I licked it. By heaven licked it! In less than a week I analyzed the pigmentation, got a formula in only thirteen attempts, and up a dye that's identical in every respect. The dye stands up even under ultraviolet."

Halley's boasting was excusable in that it was more an expression delight than of ego. He turned to Mary, surveying her critically. "And now, darling—if you'll just shuck off your duds, we'll get to work."

A little of the sudden fright within her mirrored through Mary's eyes. "You mean—"

Mark stepped close and laid a hand gently upon her shoulder. "There's still clause five," he said.

Mary stiffened. "I wish you'd stop implying that I'm afraid of this assignment. I'm just asking that it be put into plain words. I take it I'm to be dyed green?"

"Not now—not this minute," Halley said cheerfully. "There's some preliminary work. Measurements, so we'll be absolutely sure you fit the physical requirements; skin tests, so we won't be floundering around in the dark when we do the actual dying job. But there isn't too much time, darling. Get your clothes off."

Mary glanced at Mark, her look eloquent. She had no great objection to stripping before Halley, not if it came in the line of duty. There was something entirely sexless about the little chemist that made for a lack of embarrassment. But Mark...

The C4 Chief understood. "I'll run along and leave you in the Professor's hands. Come back to the office when you're through."

He left the room without looking back. Halley bent over and picked up the fallen sheet, tossing it to Mary. "You can strip behind that screen," he said unconcernedly. "Then take the other table."

Mary went behind the screen, and as she undressed she saw Halley leaning over the green girl, minutely studying a section of her breast under a large reading glass.

CHAPTER TWO

TEN MINUTES later, after exhaustive measurements had been taken, Mary also lay upon a table with Halley's high-powered glass trained upon her skin. Halley seemed delighted with what he discovered.

Halley said, "The dying job will be a cinch. The least of your worries. The important thing is whether or not you'll have the mental strength to retain your own personality under the conditioning."

"Then they plan to go—all the way?"

"Of course. Anything short of that would be more dangerous than the calculated mental risk. You see, we're in the dark concerning these people. They may have ways of learning true identities that we know nothing about. The only answer is to be the party under whose colors you're masquerading."

Mary smiled in spite of herself as Halley stepped back and laid down his instruments. "That's all for now. I'll make some lab checks, but things will work out fine."

He was now bending over the green girl, and called after Mary who was dressing behind the screen. "Oh, darling, I forgot to tell you. You'll be in bed, blindfolded, for two days. That's when we'll inject the deeper shade of green onto your irises."

Suddenly Mary wanted to get out of the room. Ready to leave, she brushed past Halley and deliberately avoided looking at the green girl.

Once in the long corridor, she stopped to compose herself. She stood for a moment biting her lip; sternly telling herself she wasn't afraid—that it was just the strangeness, the newness of the assignment. Possibly she did not convince herself, but there was no sign of faltering as she marched into Mark Clayton's office.

THERE WAS a delay, however, before she completed the act of entering. A voice over Mark Clayton's interoffice visiphone brought Mary to an unconscious halt with the well-oiled door open only slightly. Mary was not given to eavesdropping, but the incident was precipitated so suddenly that she found herself doing it without thinking. Then, a few moments having passed, she hesitated to either back away and let the door close, or to enter Mark's office. Now she became lost in the conversation beyond the door.

The President of the United States was saying, "The news from the Army is pretty bad, Mark. I get the feeling we're absolutely at the mercy of these creatures."

"They seem satisfied with what they have, sir."

The President's voice was a trifle sharp. "That sounds to me like the wrong attitude, Mark. Chicago is an American city, remember? They threw American citizens out bodily—"

"I didn't mean it that way, sir. I consider it an advantage in that it gives us time. Acceptance of the situation is of course out of the question."

The President seemed mollified. "Oh, I see. Well, you've got a point there."

"I've got more than that, sir. I've got the girl we need. Halley just phoned me that the tests are favorable. We'll have her in their camp within a week."

There was a pause. Then, "I don't know, Mark. I'd say it's a long shot; a tremendously long shot."

"Of course it is, sir—but—"

"Does she know about—the other half of the plan?"

"No. I haven't told her. By the way—what's the latest on the South American bloc? Any word?"

"None at all. It looks to me as though the fools consider this action a break in their favor—as though they are still playing Earth politics. We can't, of course, bid for a healing of the rupture. With Asia tottering in the balance, that would be suicidal."

MARY COULD visualize Mark biting solemnly upon the battered stem of his pipe. "I'd say our only hope is to solve this Chicago problem and regain our territory. For some unaccountable reason, the whole world seems to view it as our personal misfortune. They don't view it as a world threat at all."

"I think I know the reason for that."

"I'd appreciate hearing it, sir." "They think we can contain and lick it. Regardless of present alignments, we're still looked upon as the first world power. They're all afraid of us. Even Sargo wouldn't dare attack openly."

"But the longer these attackers from outer space hold Chicago, the lower our stock falls on the world market. We've got to get in and find out something about them."

"You're absolutely sure of your operator?"

"I'd back her to the hilt," Mark said.

"And you're sure complete conditioning is a good idea? What if our scanners aren't able to penetrate that ray curtain of theirs?"

"It's a calculated risk, sir. But I've checked exhaustively with our top brains on the subject. They say it can."

"Very well, Mark. I'll leave it up to you. Keep me posted."

Mary pushed open the door in exact coincidence with the fading of the president's image on Mark's video-screen. Mark looked up and gave her a brief, impersonal smile. "All finished with Halley?"

"For the time being."

"Fine. Sit down. I hope he wasn't too rough on you."

Mary dropped into a chair. "No one minds Professor Halley. He's a—I guess you'd call him a character."

"That about sums him up. Have you decided you want to take this assignment?"

"I was never in doubt."

"Then I'll really get down to brass tacks. As you've of course figured out, we plan to dress you in an attractive shade of green and send you behind the enemy lines. We've got to find out the nature of the weapons holding us helpless. We've got to get some data on the plans of those beautiful green and purple people. We've got to go on the supposition that they have a weakness. And we've got to find that weakness."

"I'll do my best."

Mark frowned, hesitated. "I want you to undergo complete conditioning, Mary. There's so much at stake. I'm not saying you couldn't achieve your objective without it, but—but we don't know these people. We don't dare underestimate their cleverness."

"I'm perfectly willing to go all out."

Mark got up suddenly, rounded his desk and took Mary's hands into his own. "Sometimes I get sick of this thing called patriotism—this doing the job in spite of heart, hell, or high water." He dropped her hands and took a quick turn around the room. "I wish you weren't an absolute natural for the job. The only agent we've got with both the looks and the brains."

Mary smiled at him, and a trace of tenderness slipped into the smile. "Let's get on with it, Mr. Clayton."

COMPLETE conditioning. Mary lay on a cot under a white sheet. Beside her lay the beautiful green girl. Between the two cots was a compact, though complicated, unit that had been rolled in on four rubber-tired wheels. It was in the complete charge of two white-coated young men who had impersonal efficiency written all over them.

One of the young men sat before a board covered with dials, a headset over his ears. He touched the dials at various times and with various pressures.

The other young man held a position at the upper ends of the cots, giving concentrated attention to the two subjects. He wore a stethoscope, which he applied to each chest periodically, checking against a large second-dial on the wall. At intervals he took from his vest pocket a pencil-light that flashed a rhythmic beat when pointed at the flesh under the subject's eyelids.

Nearby stood Mark Clayton, taking in the scene in brooding silence.

Complete conditioning. The transfer of an entire consciousness-image from one mind to another. The creation of a complete new personality in one brain pattern, superimposed over the memory, the subconscious, and the consciousness in the brain tissues of the receiving subject. The taking of a brain-picture from one skull and its secure anchoring into another.

The creation of mental twins with the aid of new science.

Mary closed her eyes and deliberately composed her features in order that the panic in her heart be hidden. She was familiar with the implications of complete conditioning, but this was her first actual experience as a receiving subject.

She comforted herself with thoughts of the scanner. It was a sure antidote. The scanner would always reflect her true personality. And when it was all over, the scanner would...

FOR THOUSANDS of sectors, the *Narkus*—great self-sufficient steel world that it was—had swung in a wide orbit through space. Unnumbered sectors, during which time the old Argans had died; new ones had been born; honored genealogies had been established.

A religion had sprung from the fiber of these people and a history supported their dignity. And the history and the religion were curiously intermingled. It was written in the book that: *In the beginning there was Argan, and much strife, because certain of the tribes became stiff-necked and contemptuous of their brothers.*

And the time when bitterness and hatred caused the tribes to split asunder and death and destruction lay over the face of the land.

And a time when evil triumphed over good and the good were driven into hiding while their gods forsook them.

And a time when the revered fathers of the beaten tribes put dirt upon their own heads and went in to the caves to pray to the gods.

And a time when the gods heard the prayer of the fathers and took them by the hand and led them to a great cave.

And a time when the gods said, "We will not forsake a just people. Call into this cave your enlightened sons. Bid them build a world of steel four hundred times larger than the little worlds in which you ride above the land of Argan. Bid them labor long and hard, and during the time of the building your gods will protect you from the hatred of your enemies.

And a time when the fathers rejoiced in this favor from the gods and called in all the good and just technicians—all the good and just scientists—all the good and just laborers who came and rejoiced also at this favor from the gods...

MARY WRITHED under the disciplinary pain of the conditioning. Her eyes opened and she saw Mark standing by. Mark? Who was Mark? Glan, that's it—not Mark. Then the sickening horror of realization.

Glan was dead.

She closed her eyes. The white-coated young man lifted her left eyelid, and for a moment she saw the room blurred and out of focus.

She heard quiet voices—voices filled with concern—but none of them was the voice of Glan.

Somebody said, "Anything wrong?"

"An overcharge."

"What does that mean?"

"It could mean any of a dozen things, but it's probably the result of too strong an ultrasonic feed. This is a delicate process, Mr. Clayton. It doesn't go by blueprint. We have to feel our way at times."

"Be careful. Please be extremely careful."

There was no answer, only the subdued hum of the conditioner and the breathing of the white-coated man leaning over Mary. Mary's legs, the muscles across her abdomen, the cords of her neck, had stiffened. Now they relaxed. The sense of peace returned...

AND A time when life in the great cave spanned several generations. But the good and the just people never lost faith in their gods and the gods kept faith with the good and the just. And this was the Second Epoch.

And a time when the new world was finished in all its mighty, steel-ribbed glory, and there was great rejoicing, although the revered fathers who had talked with the gods were long dead, and the first technicians and scientists were dust in the lower caves. But still the good and just people rejoiced because the instructions of the gods were clear. The revered fathers had written them down carefully in the book.

And a time when the book was read to the good and just people in the great rave. "Call your finest technicians into the new world which shall be called Narkus, and bid them plot a great orbit of four hundred thousand and ten segments. This orbit shall be plotted from the cosmic position of the day the revered fathers first put soil upon their heads and prayed for guidance."

And a time when this was done and all the other things were done that the gods had directed and all the good and the just people entered into the Narkus and started off on the great orbit as directed by the gods. And this was the Third Epoch.

MARY SHUDDERED as a wave of nausea brought her own personality back into her conscious mind. She heard a quiet voice: "Careful—an overcharge."

The humming of the machinery lessened. Mary opened her eyes and found them focused on the profile of the green girl lying on the cot next to her. The girl's eyes were closed and her breast rose and fell evenly under the white sheet. "Is she—suffering?" Mary asked.

"No. She is completely unconscious. The receiver is the only one who experiences any discomfort in a conditioning."

"Will she suffer any ill effects?"

"No more so than a person sitting for a photograph. We're merely taking a picture of her mind—or, rather, transplanting it."

Mary closed her eyes. "I must be a poor receiver. I'm causing you a lot of trouble."

"No, the contrary. It's going very well."

Mary wondered if Glan was still in the room. Glan? No, a different name. But who could it be except Glan? Again the hum of the machine...

CHAPTER THREE

IN THE history and heritage of the Argans—nay, even in their religion—was a time in the future when the sealed pages of the book would be opened. This was known when the *Narkus* first settled into the great orbit—was known by people who would never live to discover what the sealed pages contained.

The ones who would witness that pivotal event were called the chosen ones, and were deeply grateful for their good fortune.

The news was given out by the leaders and all the citizens of the *Narkus*—some thirty-odd thousand souls—gathered outside the central temple to hear the words of wisdom. One of the leaders opened the book and read:

"Within forty segments of the great orbit, you will come to a family of planets moving around a yellow sun. The great orbit will interlock with the orbit of one of these planets. It was so ordained when one of the revered fathers had a deep dream in which the gods spoke to him. He took the dream to the good and just scientists and it was interpreted by them and the great orbit was plotted from their interpretation of the words of the gods.

"This planet will be your future home. Thus will the Third Epoch begin.

"For full three thousand sectors, you have been trained in what you are to do. You are in the hands of your leaders. Our blessings go with you."

And there was great rejoicing among the people.

And more. Wild rumors flew thick and fast through the *Narkus*. Word was that the leaders had decided to ignore the instructions in the book and find a different world. No one knew why.

And word had it that the leaders had made contact with intelligent beings on the planet and were invited to make a home there.

The first rumor was proven groundless when the *Narkus* did set down on the huge water body on the new planet. And the second rumor was disproven when the natives gave no welcome. Surely they had not been invited.

MARY OPENED her eyes. The hum of the machine had ceased. The green girl lay sleeping on the other cot. Mary said, "I—I feel quite normal. Was the conditioning a failure?"

Only one of the white-coated specialists remained. "On the contrary. A complete success. Do you feel strong enough for a short briefing?"

"Of course."

"You are now under the scanner. As long as it is set to your brain vibration, the new personality and background will remain entirely subconscious. In short you will feel entirely normal. The scanner is effective from a distance of two hundred miles. It will remain much closer to you than that at all times.

"Certain instincts—certain commands—have been hypnoted into your subconscious which will dominate when you are under the influence of your new personality. When you are under the influence of that personality, you will have no memory of your true entity. It will be while you are under the influence of the new personality that you will acquire—or attempt to acquire—the information your superiors must have.

"At certain set times each day, your subconscious will be scanned from beyond the perimeter of the area under siege and the information recorded. During the periods of scanning; you will return to your true entity wherever you are."

The specialist paused as though making sure he had missed nothing. "Is that quite clear?"

"Yes."

"You seem doubtful."

"Over another point. I'm not convinced all this was necessary. I could have been given the scannings from this girl's mind through hypnotics. I see no reason why I shouldn't have entered the area equipped with my own entity."

"The reason for that, I believe, was your own personal safety. The invading race must be of a high order. They will have methods of checking a suspected spy. Infallible methods. To the best of our knowledge, complete conditioning defies all detection."

"I see."

"I believe Mr. Clayton is waiting for you."

PROFESSOR HALLEY was in an excellent mood. "You will step into this tub, my dear."

Mary dropped the sheet she'd held around her and slipped down into the tub of dark green liquid. Halley stood back and looked on with the air of a celebrated chef who had just finished concocting a new and savory soup.

"Twelve formulae," he chuckled. "Then the thirteenth and success. Are you superstitious, my dear?"

"No, but this stuff is pretty hot. I may be parboiled."

"No danger of that. And when you come out, you'll be the gaudiest thing outside the city limits of Chicago. The woman in skin thirteen." Halley took time out to chuckle.

He repeated the phrase. "Quite good, don't you think? I'm sharp today."

"You're always sharp, Professor. How long will this take?"

"About an hour."

Halley inserted the plugs deep in Mary's ears. Then he saw to the tubes through which she would breathe during complete submersion. The cap came next. "We'll do your scalp separately," he said. "A very delicate operation."

Then he sealed Mary's eyelids with a narrow strip of gum. This done, he pushed her completely under.

She lay there in pleasant isolation. The liquid cooled and she grew drowsy. She tried to isolate and identify the presence of the scanner ray and could not.

Then her mind went back to the conversation she'd heard outside Mark Clayton's doorway. One particular part of it flared brightly in her memory:

"Does she know about—the other parts of the plan?"

"No, I haven't told her."

This was the first time Mary had had an opportunity to ponder on the cryptic words. They could mean only one thing. There was something in this situation the high brass knew but refused to state even in private conversations. Mary's experience told her the reason for this seemingly unnecessary secrecy. In this day of brilliant scientific research, men never knew whether or not they were really alone. There were ingenious instruments. There were highly trained and conditioned spies who knew how to use the instruments.

The only place top secrets were discussed were in the soundproof, lead-lined booths in which not more than three men could sit at a time.

Yes, there was something the high brass knew that they weren't telling.

MARY WALKED up to the full-length mirror and stood gasping.

She was naked except for the brief feather costume that had been worn originally by the green girl.

But now Mary herself was the green girl. The cosmetic specialists stood by holding photos taken at various angles. Professor Halley wore a self-satisfied smirk. "A complete success in every detail. No one could possibly tell them apart. We've a right to be proud of ourselves."

Mark Clayton was standing by. He removed his pipe from his mouth to say, "We haven't got too much time. We'll give you a few hours to get used to yourself. Then we head for Chicago."

"I'm ready," Mary said. She glanced again at the mirror. "It is a rather nice color—and a nice name, too. Mara—Mara Zo."

Mark Clayton grinned ever so slightly. "Are you single, Mara? Or do you have a husband back in Chicago?"

Mary turned startled eyes. "I—I'm single, of course."

"I agree with you," Mark said, "it's a very nice name. Let's go."

TWENTY-FOUR hours later, under cover of darkness, a small group crossed an open pasture in the heart of the farmland southwest of Chicago. The group consisted of Mark Clayton, two military aides, and a beautiful woman—a woman almost naked, whose green coloring was not visible in the darkness.

"Right about here," one of the military men said. "Their screen is about a hundred feet ahead. They've got one of those bat camps over on the other side of the pasture. They'll see her lying here come dawn."

There was no time for much in the way of goodbyes. Mark squeezed Mary's hand. "This is it," he said. "You know what you've got to do. As soon as they come for you, we'll turn off the scanner. Then we'll pick you up for an hour every night at ten."

Mary returned the pressure. "Goodbye, Mark."

"So long—Mara Zo."

IT WAS very peculiar. Two *zants* were holding Mara's arms. She was standing in open country near a *zor* roost and the *zants* had her, but she could not remember where she'd been or how she'd gotten to the open country.

Both *zants* were grinning, still unable to believe their good fortune. "It's her all right," one of the *zants* said. "This is a fine day for us, Bon. The reward will be great for this one."

"It will take a great load off the minds of the leaders— getting her back. They will probably execute her immediately."

"And reward us greatly. Careful— she's full of tricks."

The first thing Mara asked herself, of course, was: *Is it safe to think?* Could she bring her mind out from behind the protection of that silly historical background for a little while and use it for that for which it was intended?

She looked off toward the *zor* roost and saw only *zants*— out in the early morning for sport on the *zors*. No *gorts* we're in evidence to pry into her brain with their powerful telepathic tentacles.

Feeling temporarily safe from them, she uncovered her mind. What could have happened? The last thing she re- membered was breaking away from a squad of *zants* taking her out for execution. Escape inside the ray-cap was impossible, so she'd used the mental key and had gone outside.

The *zants* were now hauling her across the pasture toward the big round roost. Others of their kind had stopped activities to watch. Even though she herself was a *zant,* Mara's lip twisted in contempt. The fools! The weak, spineless, mindless fools!

But Mara had no time to indulge in the luxury of a sneer. Furiously, her mind went back to her personal problems. Desperately, she probed her memory, seeking to fill the gap. But there was nothing there; nothing but the certainty that there *should* be something.

She had used the mental key—no; possibly she should go back further than that and try to establish a running continuity that would carry through...

After the white visitor—the native of this planet— boarded the *Narkus,* information had leaked out concerning his talk with the leaders, and the Resistance had flared into the open. It had been put down brutally, of course, and the leaders had had their way—the way of involving the Argans in the coming war on this planet.

THE LANDING had been made before the Resistance tried again to gain control; the results were bloody. Mara remembered hiding in the huge deserted buildings in the city—hiding until one of the small party had dropped his mental block and the mind tracers had found them.

Running—ducking here and there like hunted animals. Glan shot down—running—running; then, out through the ray-cap.

It was no use. Mara hit the memory block again. Something had happened. She was sure of that. Something had to have happened. Possibly she'd been captured and her memory pattern blocked out back to that point.

No—these strange pale people did not have the science to accomplish such things.

Mara and her captors had arrived at the *zor* roost now. Many of the *zants* had given over their sport and were packed close around in stupid wonder.

Mara's captors were being very self-important. "Stand back there, please. Stand back now."

"We have captured a very important prisoner."

"The leaders will want us to bring her to them immediately."

"Stand back."

And from the gathering, Mara could hear the low comments:

"They will be rewarded."

"...praised by the leaders."

"...given special dreams."

And Mara's heart bled for her people.

But she had little time to ponder on the broad, ancient tragedy of the *zants*. Her own worries were more pressing. While crossing the pasture, she had become aware of strange urges, new desires, and they perplexed her.

Why, for instance—with death facing her in the very near future—should she feel the urge to know what made the ray-cap work—the scientific facts behind the hypnotic blaster and the various ray-guns?

Far more important to try and escape from the two *zants* who were leading her to her doom. One of them pushed her roughly into an air-sled. They got in on each side of her while the groups around them dispersed and went back to their sport. Already several *zors*, with *zants* tight in the saddle behind the huge, leathery wings, were looping and darting above the pasture.

One *zor* bulleted straight upward until its contact-sense told it the ray-cap was close. The *zor* reversed and went into a perpendicular dive, pulling out a scant fifteen feet from the ground, to angle horizontal with a fearful neck-snapping jerk.

NOW THE air-sled lifted and started toward the cluster of tall buildings to the east. Mara turned her eyes on the *zant* at the controls. "You expect them to give you good dreams in return for my capture?"

He nodded. "Good dreams."

"But not the best."

The other *zant* leaned forward to get into the discussion. "Why not the best? You are a very important traitor."

"Because they no longer have the best dreams—or any others. The Resistance raided the boxes one night during the last uprising. We hid the dream pellets in a place of trees to the north. No one will ever be able to find them. And it will take months to make more."

The *zant* at the controls frowned. He was of a delicate violet hue and was handsome, as were all the male Argans. That was the trouble; sometimes you couldn't tell a *gort* from a *zant*, because the former often adopted the child-like, stupid attitude and bearing of the *zants*. These two were not *gorts* however; of that Mara was sure. A *gort* would never indulge in childish pleasures, such as riding *zors*.

"I am one of your kind," Mara said. "Why do you take me in to be killed?"

The *zant* at the controls thought it over, his lower lips protruding, as from intense concentration. "You caused trouble," he said finally.

"Yes—but for the benefit of all of us. The *gorts*—since the two tribes joined forces long ago—have used the *zant*s as slaves—have exploited us."

"The *gorts* are favored by the gods," the left *zant* cut in. "They built the steel world in which we crossed space. They allowed us to come with them, lest the other tribes of Argan kill us all."

"They want us in order to dominate! They really hold us in the contempt we deserve. Mara's voice deepened in bitterness as she allowed her mind to flare full force—entirely forgetful that it might be picked up by a mind tracer. "You've seen them cut us down in cold blood—you've seen how they crushed the last Resistance uprising."

"That's because the *zants* taking part were bad," the air-sled driver said in the chiding tones of a child. "The *gort* leaders know what is best. They allow us our *zors*—they give us dreams."

CHAPTER FOUR

MARA GROUND her teeth in an agony of frustration. Was it worth while trying to save a people too stupid to know they were being used? Was it merely a losing game, fighting eternally against a force too broad and too intelligent to be beaten?

"They give you bats and dream pellets," Mara said, her voice husky with contempt. "The playthings of children."

"But we like *zors* and dreams. When one likes a thing—"

"*Why* do you like them? Because the *gorts* put mind-stunting chemicals in the dream pellets. You think they give them to you because you ask for them? That's not true. The *gorts* know you will ask, but if you didn't they'd insist you take the pellets. Without them your minds would develop. That's how the Resistance was born. A group of us got together and swore to stop taking the dreams. Our minds grew strong and we could think for ourselves and see the *gorts* as they are, before they knew we weren't taking dreams. They tried to force us, but it was too late. We had built mental strength and could overcome the drugs."

The two *zants* listened stolidly. One of them said, "The *gorts* read to us out of the book. They tell us of our great heritage, of our—"

"The book!" Mara spat. "A pack of lies concocted by the *gorts*. You know what we of the Resistance think of the book? We use it for a mind shield!"

"Then we didn't come from Argan—in the beginning?"

Mara turned wearily to the *zant* seated on her left. As she did so, she noted he was paying little attention to the controls; that, or else he was slowing the sled down deliberately. A spark of hope glittered in her mind.

"Certainly we came from Argan," she said. "But most of the rest is lies. The text is colored so that even the truthful parts are twisted around."

The other *zant* hadn't seemed to be listening. Now he said, "Are you sure you stole all the dream pellets?"

"Why do you ask?"

He looked at the driver of the sled. "It just came to me. We haven't been given our ration of pellets. We should have gotten them yesterday. The *gorts* were never behind in the distribution before."

"Listen," Mara said, in sudden desperation. "Will you join the Resistance? Will you stop taking the pellets and become strong of mind? Then you'll see what the *gorts* do to your people. The knowledge comes with the new strength. You'll realize they take your women and use them like animals—for their own unspeakable pleasures—that your men are killed and tortured daily in horrible laboratories where they carry on their brain experiments."

There was no response. "Don't you *want* to grow up? Do you want to remain children until you die?"

"Are you telling the truth? Did you really steal all the dream pellets?"

Mara saw it was no use. There was a moment of silence broken only by the purr of the drive unit in the sled. Then she turned to smile at the driver. "Yes. Even the ones they give out for special merit; the ecstasy dreams they would give you for capturing me."

THIS WAS something beyond the ordinary—beyond the routine. Both the *zants* puckered their brows as they pondered it.

Mara said, "So I am in a better position to reward you for letting me go than they are for taking me in. I'll give you all the ecstasy pellets—all of them."

It was a terrible temptation for the type of minds that rode with Mara. The *zants'* eyes glowed. There was eagerness in the handsome, purple faces.

"It would be wrong," said one.

"Very wrong," the other stated.

"Ecstasy pellets. All we want."

"All we could ever use."

"You could hide them," Mara suggested, "and have dreams for the rest of your lives."

"That would be wonderful."

"Or give them to your friends and get much praise."

"Where are the pellets?"

"In the wooded land to the north. Point the sled forty-five degrees to your left. I will tell you when to change it."

"We are not agreeing, of course," the driver said firmly.

"I understand."

"No, not agreeing," the other assured her—and himself.

"We will just look at the pellets."

"Make sure they are there."

Mara promoted no more conversation. The urge to do inexplicable things was again strong within her, filling her mind. One of the strongest urges was to locate the native who had met with the leaders here. She was suddenly thirsty for knowledge concerning him; something more solid than the rumors she had heard.

Hearsay in the Resistance had it that this planet, called Earth, was not the charted destination of the *Narkus* at all; that the leaders had hove to from curiosity before going on.

While inside the atmosphere they'd made contact—or had been contacted—by this mysterious native—who sought the aid of the Argans in a strictly planetary war.

It was through this native's instructions that the landing had been made on the water near the city. Now the *gort* leaders were waiting, ready to trade the lives of many *zants* for whatever advantages they could get. Rumor had it also that the natives slipped in and out of the city at will. As a matter of fact, Mara herself had seen a pale stranger hurrying into the *gort* headquarters housed in a huge building called the Palmer House.

Too, Mara wanted to know about the weapons of the Argans; wanted to know technical details she had never cared about before. A deep-seated uneasiness laid its grip on her mind. There was something wrong—something different— some change had come over her—

"Two degrees to the left," Mara said. Then, a few moments later, "Wing over to that clump of trees. You'll find a small open space. Lower into it."

The *zant* set the sled down carefully. Then both of them jumped to the ground. They made no effort to hide their eagerness. "We'll just inspect them—make sure," one told the other.

"That's right. It wouldn't be honest to take any of them."

A HALF-SMILE of pity pulled at Mara's lips as she walked swiftly toward a thicket to the south of the platform. The *zants* followed trustingly.

Mara dropped to her knees beside a thick bush and thrust her hand in toward its roots.

"Ecstasy tablets—imagine that," one of the *zants* said. "I've only seen one in my whole lifetime."

From the corner of her eyes, Mara caught the other *zant* looking speculatively around. She knew that already he was searching for a secluded thicket in which to hide himself for the dream.

Mara turned suddenly, coming to her feet in the same motion. In her hand was a small gun.

The eyes of the *zants* widened. "A para-tube."

"We— I don't understand."

Mara pressed the switch. There was only a slight buzzing sound; no fire, no visible rays. But the two *zants* stiffened, then tipped over like a pair of beautiful purple statues. Swiftly, Mara bent down to examine them. Their flesh was hard as rock. The gun had thrown an excellent charge. She'd gotten it from a cache placed there against such an emergency as this, and the Resistance had been careful to steal only the best weapons.

Mara regarded the *zants* with a queer mixture of affection and pity. "Sleep well, my babies," she whispered, and thrust the small ray-tube into her bra—into the slight valley between her breasts.

Scarcely had she drawn her hand away when a voice said, "That's fine. Leave it there—and don't move."

TWO MEN sat in a small, lead-lined booth in the White House. One was the President himself, his face worn and haggard, his kindly eyes crow's-footed deeply. The other man was Mark Clayton.

Mark said, "We've kept a close check on him. There's no doubt in my mind that we have the right man."

"I wasn't thinking about that," the President said. "It's— well, the whole plan that worries me. I have a feeling it should have been handled differently. For instance, sending the girl in. I'm still not sure—"

Mark took the stem of his battered pipe from between his teeth. The pipe was cold out of consideration for the narrow quarters. "As I saw it," he said, "she was absolutely necessary—as a decoy. Something to occupy his mind and to make him show his hand. He'll have to get in touch—warn them. That alone will verify what are now really nothing more than suspicions on our part."

"And if we're wrong—what about the girl? Then she's been sacrificed."

"I can't agree. If that comes about, it's still an honor so far as she's concerned. A job for her country. And if this angle hadn't entered into it, the basic job is still there to be done. We need information—technical data. We need it badly."

The President sighed. "You're right, of course. Guess I'm just a small town politician. Can't get out of the habit of thinking in terms of the individual."

"I understand. But I keep remembering this is war. One of our cities is in the hands of alien invaders. Such a situation cannot be tolerated."

"You still have the male in a safe hiding place?"

"Yes—another case in point. It cost us eight American lives to get him."

"Who will handle—"

"A very competent man," Mark cut in. "We have a lot of competent men. There won't be any leaks and it won't be a complete conditioning job."

"Then you'll be gone for a while."

Mark smiled. "As short a while as possible."

"Goodbye. Take care of yourself."

"Thank you, sir. I will. Goodbye."

MARA'S first thought was that she had nothing to lose. Therefore she might as well take a chance and ignore the command. But then she turned her head and saw the *gorts*— two men and a girl—with their heat guns trained dead center.

Mara revised her thinking. She did have something to lose. The time between this moment and the hour she would be executed if she allowed herself to be taken.

By facing three heat guns with a para-tube, she would most certainly commit swift suicide. She turned slowly and the girl stepped forward. She jerked the tube roughly from Mara's bra, bruising the green skin. Mara steeled herself and did not wince.

There was no physical difference between the two *gort* males and the paralyzed *zants*. The difference was spiritual— the radiation from within. The *gorts* were sharp of eye—quick of movement. And there was a grimness in their makeup, which was the complete opposite of the open, childlike attitude of the *zants*.

Nor were they interested in dreams, although their first question concerned the pellets. One of the men came forward and took Mara roughly by the wrist. "You need to understand that it might go a little easier with you if you tell us where the pellets are. Where did your mob of traitors hide them?"

Mara smiled coldly. "So you're really worried. It *was* your total supply. And a pretty smart job on our part, wasn't it?"

"Smart? Stupid audacity, I'd say. And we'll find the pellets too. It's just a matter of time. I was just trying to show you an opening for possible leniency."

"Don't exert yourself."

The *gort* girl was regarding the stiffened *zants* with a look of disgust. She transferred the look to Mara. "Brutalizing your own kind, eh? It's about what we'd expect from a traitor. This proves the ideals you spout about are pure hypocrisy. You're interested in your own hides first, last and always."

"Are we going to stand here all day?"

One of the men motioned to the other. "Get the sled. We'll wait."

"Let's use this one," the girl said.

"We can send somebody back for these two. They'll be stiff for hours."

CHAPTER FIVE

THEY HERDED Mara into the air-sled, one of the men taking the controls while the other man and the girl kept their heat guns trained expertly. And again came Mara's thirst for technical knowledge. She stared at the heat gun in the purple man's hand. What made it work? From whence came the crackling power that burned through steel? Somewhere in the building of the leaders the information could be found. They'd certainly possess records. Mara wondered about the possibility of getting her hands on them.

Then she laughed inwardly. How foolish! She wasn't going to get her hands on anything. Before too long she would be a pinch of blackened dust from facing those same guns.

Ahead, the tall buildings of the central area by the lake sprang closer as the air-sled shot forward like a small rocket. As they rode, Mara felt the almost imperceptible tickling within her head, which indicated the crossing of a brain tracer path. Instantly, she cleared her mind and threw up a screen—just in time.

A minute passed, then the tracer came nosing back—seeking her out—seeking to check the suspicions aroused during the brief contact. It tingled for a full minute against her barrier, then went on its way.

Now the area of closely packed buildings was below. The air-sled settled onto a broad roof. Guards were there to anchor it, and Mara was led down a stairway and into an elevator.

One of the male *gorts* had remained above, leaving her in charge of the girl and the other man. Five minutes later, they faced a handsome, purple man over a huge desk. Mara cringed inwardly in spite of herself, for this was Morn—one of the most dreaded of the leaders—Morn, in charge of military operations and the putting down of rebellions.

Tales were told of him—his savagery with both men and women; savageries in both business and pleasure. Mara could well cringe.

Morn looked her over with an almost impersonal contempt. He allowed his eyes to rest upon her loins and then her breasts with what was obviously studied insult. He was silent for some time, dominating the room with his silence. If the captors of Mara expected praise, they were doomed to disappointment.

WITHOUT glancing their way, Morn finally snapped, "Throw her into the jail downstairs with the rest of her kind. When we get a little time we'll have a grand killing. I'd like a few more gathered in first, though."

Mara had been waiting for queries relative to the location of the dream pellets. Either Morn had already found them—through mental weakness on the part of a captured Resistance member—or else his silence regarding them was a tribute to Mara. Possibly he knew it was a waste of time trying to break this girl down.

Mara was taken from the office and back to the elevator. Her captors opened the door just in time to block the entrance of a native—a small, worried-looking little man with pouting lips and an almost feminine cast to his eyes.

Entirely preoccupied with his own thoughts, the native brushed past the trio. But a peculiar thrill ran through Mara. Her interest in the native flared even above thoughts of her coming death.

Then he was gone, the door was closed, and Mara was being led toward the elevator.

Her second thrill came in a long, low passageway—underground—which seemed to lead into another of the tightly packed buildings. There, the trio came upon four *zants*—two males and two females—busy scrubbing the stone floor.

But only apparently busy. Mara knew immediately the business of cleaning was only an act. She knew also that Glan had not been killed—or even captured. Because Glan was one of the four—the one kneeling near a pail over which was laid a scrubbing cloth.

The rescue was achieved with cold mathematical precision. At just the right instant, Glan reached under the cloth, into the bucket, and came forth with a heat gun. As though having been carefully rehearsed, the remaining three lunged forward, hitting the two guards low and knocking them to the floor.

Mara, her help not needed, plunged on past Glan, out of the heat gun's range. The three rescuers, after knocking down the guards, reversed directions with agile speed, to roll, sprint, and crawl out of range also.

Then they turned to watch Glan do his deadly work. While the guards clawed desperately for their weapons, Glan's gun spurted a thin stream of white-hot flame. The bodies of the captors shriveled under the intense heat.

But they made no outcry—because Glan's heat gun stream cut first at their throats, severing their heads—sending their heads rolling on the hard floor.

SWIFTLY, silently, Glan continued his terrible work, spraying the heat stream, reducing the captors' bodies to smaller and smaller piles of residue until nothing was left but some charred bone.

Now Glan snapped off the gun, and the bone residue was quickly swept up by the other three Resistance members and deposited in pails. And so carefully had Glan used the heat gun that not a mark showed on the stone floor.

The grim, savage annihilation now finished, the party took up their buckets and moved off down the corridor, their skill and forethought demonstrated in the fact that a bucket had been provided also for Mara.

They did not move swiftly; rather, their progress was remarkably slow; their eyes dull and lifeless; their manner almost that of children.

Down, down they went, ever deeper into the basements and subbasements of the huge building. Nothing was said— no words passed—as each member of the group played a part.

In a lower passage they encountered three *gort* guards, all male, each carrying a brace of heat guns and each wearing a deep scowl.

The *zants* shuffled to a halt, stepped aside, and stared dully at the *gorts*. Mara's acting was as clever and convincing as that of the others. But in her heart was a greater tension—a tension coming from long hours of fear and a sense of anticlimax. She hoped the *gorts* would continue on their way. She was disappointed.

The lead guard hesitated, then came to a halt. "Where are you going?"

A long moment of silence, after which Glan mumbled, "To empty the pails. The water gets dirty. We must have fresh water."

The *gort* grunted contemptuously, then shrugged. As the trio moved on, Glan broke the silence again.

"Good dreams."

The *gorts* did not deign to acknowledge the greeting, nor even to look back. When they were out of sight, Glan indulged in the luxury of a grin. "It's not far now," he whispered, and the shuffling forward was continued.

They came to what appeared to be a grating over a sewer drain. "Here," Glan said, with urgency.

The two males lifted the grate. Then the members of the rescue party lowered themselves swiftly down through the small opening. Mara followed Glan, to find utter darkness, terrible odors, and a distasteful softness under foot.

"It will smell better before long," Glan said. He took Mara's hand and led her through the darkness to a place where lines of light showed in the wall. Glan tapped on wood and a crude panel opened into a large cement room.

Glan turned and smiled at Mara. "Welcome," he said. "Our new headquarters. The natives had a railroad under their city once. It went into disuse and was apparently forgotten. The *gorts* don't know it's here."

Glan's manner changed now. Gone was the impersonal ruthlessness. While the other Resistance members went swiftly away to find business elsewhere, Glan put his arms around Mara and laid his head on her shoulder. Then he raised his head and Mara did the same thing, laying her head eagerly against Glan's neck.

"I missed you," she murmured. "I thought you were dead."

Before Glan could reply, Mara did a strange, unexplainable thing. She drew Glan's head down and placed her lips against his. She saw his eyes widen in blank surprise while—far above, and unheard by either of them—the clock in the Wrigley Tower boomed ten times.

MARY STIFFENED as she realized she was in the arms of a strange, purple man; that her lips were against his lips. She was disturbed by the feeling that she was in those arms from choice. She was on the verge of jerking away when memory came to her rescue.

Somewhere out beyond the deadly perimeter of the space invader's invisible shield, a mind scanner had been turned on—a scanner tuned to her individual brain wave.

Smothering her surprise by gargantuan effort, she smiled at the violet man and began drawing back very slowly. He made no effort to hold her. His face reflected surprise, bewilderment.

"Why did you do that?"

"Do what?"

"Place your lips against my lips. What does it mean?"

An unconscious blush warmed Mary's face, hidden fortunately by the apple-green complexion. Swiftly she realized there must have been a moment of merging between the two personalities as the scanner brought her own to the fore. A merging in which the inclination of one governed the instinctive physical actions of the other.

"I kissed you," she told him, smiling archly.

"Kiss? What is kiss? What does it signify?"

"I—I saw the natives do it while I was away."

ONLY HALF of Mary's mind was centered on the conversation. The other half was busy realizing the scanner had begun its work. She wondered if it was getting any information of value. Where had she been? What had she done? Who was this purple man whom she had just kissed?

Of course the scanner was taking all this information out of her subconscious, but that did her little good personally. She sensed, however, that this must be a first meeting between Mara and someone she loved. It had all the urgency of a first meeting. Had any confidences been exchanged? Had any information been given back and forth?

She hoped not, and she knew definitely that none must be exchanged until the scanning hour had passed. The face of the violet man had cleared somewhat of surprise. Rather, the surprise had been pushed into the background by more pressing emotions. "Tell me," he said eagerly. "Where did you go? What happened?"

In Mary's mind was the desperation of not having the least idea. She contrived a smile and passed a hand lightly over his face. The face was feather-smooth. "No—you tell me first."

"Very well. When we got trapped out there in the woods—"

The trap Mary was thinking of was the one she'd fallen into herself—right here in this strange room. Any information he gave her would be lost from the standpoint of personal value. He must be sidetracked for an hour.

Mary knew of but one possible way to do this. She would steel herself to it, she thought—wondering vaguely at the same time just how much steeling would be necessary; and how much skill would be needed to ward off the ultimate. She took a deep breath and smiled, cutting the purple man off by laying a finger over his lips.

"Can't it wait, darling? It's been such a long time?"

He frowned. *"Darling?* That's a new term. It wasn't in the hypno-indiction they gave us on the language."

"I heard that from the natives, too. It's a love term. It is used by those dear to each other. Did you like the kiss?"

"The kiss?"

"The meeting of the lips. When I saw it, it looked…interesting."

She drew his head close and repeated the kiss, hoping it would serve to keep this peculiar man's mind diverted. If she had any doubts, they must have come from underestimating her own ability in that direction. The man caught on quickly.

Mary felt a moment of panic. She could divert this fervent character with a new trick—maybe a couple of tricks, characteristic of the races on an individual planet. But the ultimate end was no doubt the same on all planets. And maybe he knew a few tricks of his own.

Mary smiled and put her arms around the violet man's neck and kissed him again. He was getting the knack of it; getting the knack too quickly to suit Mary.

I wonder who he is? she thought.

CHAPTER SIX

MARK CLAYTON stood under the dim light of a sickle-moon and inspected his squad. There were four of them. They were—as was Mark himself—almost without clothing and expertly stained in a beautiful shade of violet.

And there was some of the griping to which all men of military bent are entitled. "If we had to be invaded, why didn't the Eskimos do it. I feel like a jay bird."

"Quit moaning. You'll probably be dead in a week."

"Maybe so—but I'll bet I'm *warm* then."

"Quiet," Mark said. "Final briefing."

The men came closer. Mark said, "The initial scanning of the agent already inside reveals she saw our boy entering an office in the Palmer House. It didn't reveal much else except that she's located in the basement of that building—the agent, that is.

"As you know, our technicians have found some tunnels in their lethal curtain. The openings aren't large enough for invasion purposes and seem to be caused by certain rock formations. In spots where the surface is rocky, the curtain doesn't quite touch the ground. Our experts are studying this further, but that's not our affair. While they're studying, we wriggle in under the curtain and try for several objectives. One—we'd like to kidnap our boy and get him out of there so we could score a big win in the way of world opinion. Second—I've got a relay on the scanner. It will be lifted on signal so we can find our agent and be on tap to take advantage of any information she uncovers with the aid of the underlying personality."

Mark stopped speaking. There was a pause before one of the men growled. "Mother naked, and not even a table fork to fight with."

"We have to go unarmed. There's no place on your person to hide a weapon. This is a battle of skill and brains— not weapons. We wouldn't have a chance with ours against theirs, anyhow."

Mark paused. "Any questions?"

THERE were none. The men moved in single file toward a rocky knoll out across the flat land. They reached the knoll and found a single technician squatting there awaiting them. In the dim light a chalk-marked path could be seen winding over the rock pile, following the line of a depression caused by some underground fault.

"That's it," the technician said. "You crawl along that line and you'd better scratch the hell out of your bellies rather than raise your fannies an inch more than necessary."

"Ouch," one of the men muttered in anticipation.

The technician seemed fascinated. "Lord—but you're a gaudy lot. Hope the rains don't come and wash your purple lipstick off."

"It's on for good," one of the men countered. "We caught one of them walking rainbows and copied the color of his underwear. It won't come off."

"You guys are going to freeze your—"

Mark had been studying the contour of the hill. "All right men," he cut in. "Let's hit it. I'll go first."

"Happy landings," the technician said lightly. But there was a tightness to his lips—a tension in his muscles giving the lie to his outward casualness.

Mark went down on the cold rock and started wriggling forward. The rock scratched cruelly, but this annoyance was shouldered out by the knowledge that death lay a scant inch above the highest point of his anatomy.

He did not look back, but he knew the men had fallen in behind him—four segments of a human snake. Slowly he wriggled forward. The air was cool, but sweat beads appeared on his forehead.

It seemed hours later that he cleared the rock knoll but he kept on going, belly down, across the open pasture—land beyond. One hundred yards in, he decided he must take a chance. That or crawl on his belly clear through the suburbs and into the Loop. Slowly he came to his feet.

Turning, he looked back to see the three prone figures close behind him. "It seems to be all right," he said.

But his mind and eyes were upon a single still form lying in the pathway on the knoll, rearward. The other three men came to their feet and looked backward also. There was a period of dead silence; silence one of the men finally broke with the grim remark: "Joe must have stuck his fanny up."

By common consent, they turned away. Nothing could be done for Joe. It would be suicide to approach and touch the still form.

"What's on the agenda now, Chief?" one of the men asked, turning away.

"We look around for a bat roost. There's one about a mile south of here."

"What for?" There was bewilderment in the voice.

"To get a ride to the Loop. On the basis of the memory pattern we picked up on the scanner, we four are going to be *zants*. That's new information. It seems the subject we captured had a pretty strong mental block. All we got back in Washington was a history of their trip across space that we know now was mostly fiction."

"*Zants.* That's a hell of a name. It rhymes with ants in pants."

"There seem to be two cliques in this setup. The ups and the downs. The *zants* are the downs and the *gorts* are in the saddle."

"Speaking of saddles—they got any on those damn bats?"

"You shouldn't have too much trouble. The main thing to remember is to: look stupid—feel stupid—be stupid. That makes you a *zant.* If we run into trouble, just let your mouth hang open while I do the talking. Let's go."

"Just the opposite of the razor ad," somebody said, and the party started off across the rolling land.

THE TIMING had been arranged so that the sportsmen might possibly have not yet arrived. There had been nothing in the scannings to indicate this one way or the other, but it seemed logical.

They arrived at the huge round roost, and Mark allowed himself a moment to wonder at the ingenuity necessary in the swift assembly of the globes. Then he gave off wondering as a *zant* lying asleep by the entrance to the roost came erect, rubbing his eyes.

Mark was tensely alert. There could be trouble here—and danger; possible detection even before the foray had gotten a good start. Nothing in the scannings had indicated whether or not the *zors* were individually possessed or were common property; whether permits were needed, or whether there were set hours for the sport.

Observation had indicated some riding was done at night. Mark moved on that assumption.

The sleepy *zant* said, "You've come for a ride?"

"We got restless—couldn't sleep. We made up a party." Mark stood poised on his toes awaiting negative reaction. There was none. The *zant* yawned again. "I'll wait for the yellow sun to come up," he said. Then he lay back down and went to sleep.

Mark motioned and the party pushed on into the roost. Dim light bulbs on the walls gave sufficient illumination to show rows of great ugly birds, remindful of vultures gone wild in growth, sleeping on bars bisecting the globe.

"No saddles," one of the men whispered, "but there are a lot of bridles on these pegs."

"I wonder how you get them to come?"

"Maybe you pull the rope on their leg. See? They've all got a rope hanging down. We can reach the bottom ones."

One of the party was doubtful—highly so. "Why wouldn't it be smarter to just walk into town?"

Mark replied. "Because we might run into trouble. We don't know the setup well enough. But we do know they ride these things all over and don't seem to be challenged."

Mark went forward, grasped one of the hanging ropes and tugged at it. The bird took an ugly head from beneath its wing, looked down, and croaked an obscenity. "Come on, boy—come on," Mark crooned.

IT ALMOST appeared as though the bird shrugged in resignation. It didn't, of course. It merely hopped from its perch and stood waiting with complete docility while it croaked swear-words in *zor* language.

"Hand me a bridle," Mark said.

The bridle was pushed forth and Mark held it up. The bird opened its beak; but whether to yawn or receive the bit wasn't entirely clear. Mark slipped in the bit and the *zor* lowered its head exactly like a well-trained horse.

"I should have known they'd be well-trained," Mark muttered. "These *zants* wouldn't be able to handle them otherwise."

Having set the pattern, Mark surveyed—five minutes later—his squad lined up in the pasture, each somewhat fearfully astride a bird, hard behind its wing roots. He climbed onto his own bird and raised his hand. "Follow me," he called, and dug in his heels.

The *zor* gave forth an indignant cuss-word and flailed the air with wings that lifted it into a smooth upward glide. One after another, the rest followed.

Over the treetops, Mark experimented with the bridle, hauling back on the bit. Immediately, the *zor* leveled off and skimmed swiftly eastward. Mark risked turning to look backward. Everything seemed to be going smoothly. Swinging his eyes forward, he picked out familiar landmarks in the semidarkness below and strove to pierce the gloom for a first sight of the tall Loop buildings.

Then an odd interior tickling penetrated his consciousness; a tickling seemingly inside his skull. It resembled nothing he had ever before experienced, but his instincts sounded a warning; his instincts didn't like it.

That in itself was enough to generate an additional alertness. Therefore he was waiting, tense and expectant, when the hum of an approaching drive unit cut through the sky. There was a hostile tinge to the sound.

Then, the clumsy-looking flying platform was upon them. A harsh voice barked: "Set your birds on the platform. You have ten seconds. Do as we say or we'll burn the lot of you."

MARA LOOKED into Glan's eyes and experienced a feeling of having had a mental lapse. It was peculiar. Had some unknown experience outside the ray-cap affected her mind?

Glan leaned forward and placed his lips on hers. Mara jerked back, startled. "What—what are you doing?"

He gazed at her, slack-jawed. "What do you mean—what am I doing? You showed me how."

Something told Mara not to press the point. Deeply troubled, she said, "We've been wasting time. Tell me what has been happening since I saw you last."

Glan released her and backed away, shrugging. "Very well. As I was saying, when we were trapped in the woods and you broke through the wave-cap, I fell over a rock and was sprawled out helpless."

"I thought they'd killed you."

"Falling probably saved my life. They captured me and began asking questions about the dream pellets. About fifteen minutes later, one of our roving squads came to my rescue. We gave you up for lost until today when the word came down you'd been seen going into the military leader's office. Then we laid our plans quickly."

Glan stopped speaking and stared at Mara curiously. "You've changed somehow. I can't quite put my finger on it, but you are...different. What happened during the segment you were away?"

It was Mara's turn to be startled. "The segment?"

"More than that—closer to one and a micro. What happened?"

"I—I can't remember. There is a complete gap between the moment I looked back and saw you lying on the ground, and the time I was seized by the *zor* roost. I don't know what happened."

Glan scowled. "I'd say they'd done something to you— something to your mind. But you're no different, really. And besides, they haven't the skill."

"Tell me what happened here?"

"They've been trying desperately to get the dream pellets back. They're afraid of trouble before new ones can be brewed. Already we've lost seven members to the heat guns."

Mara leaned forward and laid a hand on Glan's arm. "That native—have you found out anything about him?"

"Nothing more than we knew; that he comes in and goes out under guard to have talks with the leaders. We think he's trying to get technicians to go to some far section of this world and train the natives in making our weapons. Our leaders are holding back for several reasons. They don't think it wise to give out the secrets, and they are wondering—if the natives are so stupid—why they can't take over the world themselves."

"The fools, there aren't enough Argans to do that regardless of our weapons. We've hardly enough to hold this miserable little bit of land."

"The native has them about convinced of that. He tells them, according to our secret scanners, that there are over a billion people on this planet."

MARA'S INTENSITY increased. "Glan—isn't it time to strike—make a stand? Let's gather all our forces and try to take the Palmer House. We'd catch them by surprise because we've never made a real attack. They expect us to keep on sniping."

Glan smiled again. "We've needed your enthusiasm, Mara. We've missed it a great deal."

Mara paused. Again those unreasoning urges. Was it a sharpened instinct speaking deep within her? Or something else. She said, "Glan, we must gather up all our hidden weapons and put them in one place. We must do it immediately. They're of no value spread all over the country."

"Where will we put them?"

"With the dream pellets. The *gorts* haven't found the pellets, so that must be a pretty good place."

The violet-colored man got up and began pacing the floor. Suddenly he stopped and faced her. "Oh, what's the use, Mara. You're the only really strong one in the Resistance. The rest of us are permanently stunted by the dream pellets; secretly we long for them, and I know many would go back with the slightest excuse. Let's give it up. We weren't meant to overcome the *gorts.*"

Mara sprang to her feet, eyes blazing. "We won't give up. In fact, we're closer than ever. I have a feeling something will happen, Glan. We mustn't quit now. We can beat them and take the *Narkus*. Find an uninhabited world as we were meant to do."

"We couldn't run the *Narkus* if we had it."

"No—but we can make the *gorts* run it for us."

Glan threw up his hands in despair. "Why, even now I think there is treachery in our own ranks. I wouldn't be surprised if our own side turned us in."

There was irony in the fact that the secret knock sounded that very moment on the panel. The door opened automatically from release by an attacked mechanism. Four members of the Resistance entered the room, followed swiftly by three *gort* guards. "There they are," one of the *zants* said. "And remember—the four of us get complete pardons for turning them in."

CHAPTER SEVEN

THE *GORTS* on the flying platform would have been amazed to know in advance how small a chance they had. Their disadvantage came from over-confidence, from disbelieving the scanner.

They watched the four riders swing their *zors* in toward the platform. The clumsiness of the riders should have been a warning, but the *gorts* saw only what were obviously four *zants* out for a night ride. Their plan was to frighten them, as befit men of authority, and let them go.

Mark and his men dismounted, acting out the role of stupidity to perfection. This until they were within arm's reach of the *gorts*. And it was then that the intruders learned what it small chance they had.

The struggle was short and furious, but the fury was mainly on the side of Mark and his men. In a matter of seconds, one of the *gorts* had a broken leg and a ruptured pelvis. Another was unconscious from a split skull. A third screamed at the pain of an arm broken at the socket, and the fourth stood uninjured, in stunned surprise staring at his own gun in the hands of Mark.

"Don't hurt this one," Mark said. "I want to ask him some questions."

"What if he doesn't speak English," one of the men wanted to know.

The *gort* was no coward, basically. Mark saw the purple eyes light up in the rays from the pilot board on the platform.

"I want to know where your arsenal is," Mark said.

The *gort* stared in simulated wonder; then pointed to his own lips.

"Don't give us that," Mark said. "You were all hypno-conditioned to our language. Talk."

One of Mark's men stepped forward. "I'll make him talk."

Mark stepped back. The man moved in swiftly. His hands made swift motions, almost too fast to follow. The *gort* doubled over, emitting a choked scream. "He asked you a question," the man said.

"We have no central arsenal except on the *Narkus*. And that's really not an arsenal. It's a manufacturing plant."

"Does the ray-cap emanate from a central point?"

"No," the *gort* moaned, holding his stomach. "It comes from twenty-five hidden outlets around the circle. You'd never find them. Besides—who are you? From the Resistance?"

THE MAN who had opened the *gort's* mouth grinned wickedly. "You've no idea how big a resistance, bub." He turned to Mark. "What now, Chief?"

Mark didn't answer for a full twenty seconds. He stood staring at the skyline over the Loop. Then he snapped his fingers. "I think I've got it. The big answer!"

"Shall we dump these rats overboard?"

"No. We need this platform and one *zor*—no, wait a minute." Mark stepped to the control panel and studied it swiftly. "We won't need a *zor*. This thing has radar. Hook the four birds together by their reins and put a *gort* on each one—"

"A *gort*? You mean that's the name of these purple characters?"

"Yes. You—" Mark pointed to the able-bodied leader. "Get on the front bird. We'll strap the others into place with the hand straps and then you're on your own."

Several minutes later, the *zors* spread their wings and slipped off into space like an aerial pack train. As soon as they had cleared the platform, Mark returned to the control board. "This doesn't look too complicated," he said.

He moved one of the control rods. The platform swung too far around. He made an adjustment and the platform purred toward the Loop skyline—dark against the false dawn.

One of the men opened his mouth to speak. Mark gestured. "Quiet—there's something coming in."

They knew Mark was now listening to the tiny receiver built into a silver-lined pocket near the base of his skull. They were silent for several minutes while Mark listened and the platform slid toward the Loop.

"The scanning has been completely analyzed," Mark said finally. "Things begin to look up—maybe. We've got to locate some people, but first we follow through on the brainstorm I just got."

Mark found the platform controls relatively simple. He angled up and went over the Loop at a high altitude while he and his men shivered in the cold night air. Then he angled down sharply.

He had been surprised at the lack of alertness from below; surprised that he was allowed to come down to the surface of the lake without being challenged. The platform touched the surface and Mark braked the unit almost to a halt, allowing it to inch slowly forward toward open water. When the radar clicked, he allowed it to move another ten feet, then stopped it completely.

"Hold on the alert 'til I get back," he said. "I want to check something. I won't be gone more than five minutes." With that he dived overboard. He swam some few feet further toward open water, then went under in a flurry of purple legs.

AS THE WATERS of Lake Michigan closed over his head, he felt the peace of utter isolation. But he had not come here for peace. He swam lakeward with long, even, underwater strokes until he judged he could safely go no further. Then he reversed and went back as he had come.

The going got tough toward the end. His heart pounding in his ears sounded like a series of explosions. Finally he could stand it no longer and shot to the surface. The fact that he was still alive to take in a gulp of blessed air told him he had come up inside the ray-cap. And he'd learned what he'd wanted to learn.

Also, he now learned something else. The explosions in his ears had not been his pounding heart. A spotlight from above was centered on the platform—rather, on the place the platform had been. Now there was nothing there but a spot of boiling, steaming water. And the heat was fast spreading in all directions; so swiftly that Mark, well outside the circle of the spotlight, found himself taking a warm bath.

He turned north and started moving away with long, powerful strokes. He had gone perhaps fifty feet when a voice, close by on his left, called out, "That you, Chief?"

Mark recognized the man as he pulled close. "Where are the others?"

"Gone. Crisped down to nothing. They didn't give any warning. They just blasted away. I took a long jump and was lucky. They got it right there on the platform."

Mark said nothing. There was nothing to be said. He continued swimming northward and the last man in his squad fell in beside him. "Where we going, Chief?"

"To a place up by the river mouth—a location given me in the scanning report. I want to look it over."

They swam for an hour and were not challenged, and came finally to a place where the still, dark hulks of several old-model submarines reared into view. The early false dawn was fast becoming reality now, and Mark increased the beat of the stroke to a point where his companion was laboring.

Then the submarines were above them. Mark rounded the first one and went in beside it to the hidden ramp, waited for the other to come up beside him.

"Let's rest a while, Chief. I'm about beat."

"Sure," Mark said. "We want to be ready. Don't know what we'll find inside."

Their heavy breathing had subsided somewhat when Mark said, "You stay here. Cover my rear. I'm going inside."

HE WENT up the ramp on tiptoe. Dim light came from the hatch in the conning tower. Mark peered inside. All was quiet. After a minute he went quietly down the ladder. Halfway down he stopped abruptly as he came within sight of two purple males and a green female asleep on cots. This was a breach of conduct, he was sure. At least one of them should have been awake.

But he was glad of that breach. It gave him the opportunity of making a quiet exit. He went out as he had come—tiptoed out of earshot and took a tiny transmitter from under his loincloth.

There was no necessity of setting it or establishing contact. He knew the people waiting for him to come in wouldn't be sleeping. He spoke in a whisper, "How long since you scanned me?"

The reply came instantly into the receiver in his skull. "An hour and a half, sir."

"Then the hunch I had was right. I've proven it out since. Pass the word along to the proper authorities. But tell them to hold up until I give the word. I haven't been able to go ahead on Project Friendship yet. I'll report."

"Yes, sir."

"And throw the scanner on 497X immediately."

"Yes, sir."

"That's all."

"Good luck, sir."

Mark put his transmitter back into its hiding place where it had already chafed off a sizeable piece of skin.

MARY AWOKE with a start. But there was a hand over her mouth, so her cry was smothered in her throat. She opened her eyes to see a handsome purple face close to her own. She tensed her muscles for a struggle.

But then the purple man spoke, whispered into her ear: "It's Mark. Quiet! I've come to help you. Let's get outside quietly."

They went to the ramp where Mark's companion sat hunched over. He looked up startled. "It's all right," Mark said. The man sank back.

"Mark!" Mary whispered. "I don't understand. What are you doing here?"

"I came in to follow anywhere you led through this damn maze, and to cash in on any information you got. That was part of the original plan, you know. But I couldn't tell you earlier. Didn't want it in your mind in case they scanned. But now we have to work together."

"Did I get anything important?"

"Plenty. There's a Resistance here. The top men sitting on the majority—holding them down through a mind stunting process. Some of this lower mob—*zants* they're called—have kicked over the traces. I've got a plan, but you've got to stay under the scanner for a while."

"It will be a pleasure," Mary said. "And you know something?" She swayed close to him. "I'm damn glad to see you. If that's unladylike—make the most of it."

He grinned and kissed her swiftly. Then, "What's your layout?" he asked.

"There's a purple male I seem to hang close to. I think he's Mara's sweetheart. He's in the Resistance."

"I want to talk with him. Let's go inside. Do you get my pitch, or do you need briefing?"

"I get it. Let's go."

Mark glanced down at his subordinate. "Cover our rear."

Mary went down the conning ladder and Mark followed her.

ONCE INSIDE, Mark awoke the men, then stepped back, watching them narrowly. One evinced great guilt almost instantly. Mark quickly centered his attention upon the other.

Mary said, "Wake up, I have news. This is one of the natives. He came through the ray-cap to help us beat the *gorts.*"

The purple man stared in blank surprise. Mark said, "Hello, Glan." He checked the man's face for reaction and the reaction was satisfactory. "Mara has been telling me about you and the Resistance. We kept it secret until now, so you wouldn't have it on your mind if you were scanned. We will help you defeat your enemies and thus defeat our own."

Glan had nothing to say. He was still bewildered. He looked to Mara for guidance. "We got the guns here in time then," he said. "Is that what you had in mind, Mara, when you said we should bring them here?"

"Of course," Mary smiled. "But there are other things to be done. We must cut off the ray-cap."

Glan frowned. "But, Mara—you know that's impossible. We'd be killed before we could—"

Mark knew, of course, that Mary was groping. She'd groped in the wrong direction. "Mara is just over-enthusiastic," Mark said. "It isn't necessary to cut off the ray-cap. But one other thing would help. Is there any guard against the hypno-ray?"

Glan was getting more bewildered with each passing minute. "Of course." He looked at Mara. "Haven't you told him?"

"We were discussing other things," Mark said, thinking how similar this was to walking on eggs. "Besides, I'd rather get that sort of information from a man. It's probably too technical for a woman to understand." Mark wished fervently that Mara's ego didn't submerge completely when the scanner was turned on Mary. It was the big flaw in the complete conditioning theory. No information could be scanned from the conscious mind if it was information gleaned by another ego.

Glan was still frowning. "There's nothing very technical about it. In an area of this size, two high-frequency cross-beams will nullify the hypno-ray."

Mark rushed on, trying to keep the purple man off balance. "Another thing. A rumor must get to the *gorts* that we've solved the ray-cap and intend to attack from the air. Is there a solution to the ray?"

Glan shrugged, his troubled eyes still on Mary. "I don't know. They say there's a solution to everything."

"Here's what must be done," Mark said. "I think you'd better alert the Resistance and have them come here in ones and twos to get arms. Then you go to the *gort* headquarters and confess to being a Resistance man. But you've repented and are bringing them the information about the ray-cap and the coming attack. In order to clinch it, you can tell them where the dream pellets are—that is, after we've gotten the guns out of here."

CHAPTER EIGHT

MARY LOOKED at Mark, then swiftly hid the surprise in her face. What on earth were dream pellets? she wondered. It was Mark who sensed the true situation. This *zant* did not reflect the personality pattern found in the scannings. Therefore, he must have succumbed to temptation and was even now groggy from the dream-drug. That would account for his heavy-mindedness.

"They probably won't even scan you," Mary said. "If they do, can you throw up a barrier?"

"I—I don't know. I could try."

Mark could see that this purple man's acquiescence came from his love for Mara, his fear of displeasing her. He strove to rush the thing. "Then it's settled. Why don't you get going right away? Just leave everything else to us."

A few minutes later, they stood on the ramp. Glan had been dispatched to the Palmer House with instructions to present his revelations in exactly three revolutions of the Wrigley clock.

The other *zant* was sent out to call the Resistance in to pick up weapons.

Alone with Mark and his subordinate. Mary surveyed them thoughtfully. Then she said, "I'll handle the weapon dispersals. You two get some sleep. If you don't, you'll keel over from exhaustion."

"There are things to be done. We've got to arrange to get our hands on a friend of ours—the man who walks in and out of Chicago as though it was his own personal bathroom."

Mary glanced up quickly, but asked no questions. "Nothing can be done about that now. You've got to have some rest."

Mark yawned. "Maybe it's a good idea. We'll crawl into one of the other subs so we're out of the way. Call us if we're needed—and in two hours in any case."

Mark and his one-man squad found cots in the third submarine to the west. If they were worried about inability to rest, they had little time for it. They were asleep in a matter of seconds. The last thought in Mark's brain was:

I wonder if any of us will be alive three hours from now?

Not that it mattered much. He was too tired to care.

MARK AWOKE with a sense of lateness. He awakened his subordinate and climbed out of the submarine. Ice water coursed through his veins as he glanced at the Wrigley clock and saw the hands standing at eleven o'clock. Eleven o'clock. Four hours had elapsed since they'd descended that ladder.

Mark swung his eyes in a circle. There was no living thing in sight. The city, from where be stood, was utterly deserted. No one—white, green, or purple, walked the streets. It looked like a ghost town.

Mark leaped from the conning tower and ran down the ramp to the pier. His sense of alarm increased, even as he came to the ramp of the other submarine, and he was not as cautious as he should have been. So he found himself standing there looking into the barrel of a queer-looking gun.

There was only one person in sight. Mary was gone. None of the space intruders could be seen. The man in sight was a native.

The man said, "Good day, Mr. Clayton. I've been waiting for you."

Mark said, "And greetings to you, Professor Halley. I surmised as much."

Professor Halley had changed a great deal. Gone was the half-feminine lightness of manner for which he had been famous. Gone was the soft, humorous light in his eyes; replaced now by a flintiness that bespoke the egomaniac.

"You don't seem surprised," Halley said.

"No. We've known about you—to some extent—for some time. And how is your friend Sargo? Planning to conquer any other worlds?"

Halley snarled, the snarl showing that he could carry light repartee just so far; that his deadly earnest fanaticism, when outside the bonds of necessary caution, had to come uppermost.

"You fools," he grated. "You utter fools! How long did you think your inane and childish policy of individual freedom could last? Don't you realize that therein you sowed the seeds of your own destruction?"

"Tell me more," Mark said. His eyes were on Halley's gun; his thoughts on the possibilities of overcoming him.

"Certainly. But first, tell your man to continue his descent. Otherwise I'll be forced to blow his legs to dust."

MARK GLANCED upward and the subordinate came sullenly down the ladder. He had been standing on a center rung awaiting developments.

"That's better."

"Yes—we've known for some time that we had a rotten spot in our apple barrel."

Halley's eyes glowed. "Then why did you let it remain?" he asked, too interested in that point to take issue with the insult.

"Because the damage you could do could be estimated. We had you pretty well contained and we knew where you were. That was the main point. Anything you've done in this project could have been done by someone else. If we'd picked you up, Sargo would have gotten another boy. And we wouldn't have known what boy."

Halley sneered. "You are making an excellent job of saving face. An amazingly nonchalant piece of second-guessing. Tell me—what did you really know of Project Undermine."

"That I suppose is Sargo's code-phrase for world-treachery?"

"I asked you a question."

"We knew very little for sure, but we surmised a great deal. That either you or Sargo contacted the space invaders and invited them to roost on a piece of our territory. That he plans to use their invasion as a means of making us lose worldwide face. That he hopes, in the near future, to throw a world alliance against us. The United Stales of America against the east, the west, the north, the south."

"You hit it exactly. Of course, it was no great feat of projection. You merely took our aims and conceded that we could accomplish all of them. Your nation is doomed, Clayton."

"Then you don't consider it your nation also?"

"Of course not—in the sense you refer to. It shall be my nation, of course, but as a squirming little community to hold under my thumb."

"Would you mind telling me what happened to the people I left here?"

"The people?" The narrowing of Halley's eyes, and the slight start, told Clayton what he wanted to know. By a stroke of great good fortune, the weapons had been distributed before Halley nosed out the hiding place. Otherwise, he would certainly have apprehended a few of the *zants*.

"What did you do with them?"

"If you refer to the green lady, she is in custody. As a matter of fact, you'll see her soon." Halley got to his feet. "Enough of this. We are going to take a little walk." He motioned toward the ladder. "You gentlemen first. And if you have any idea of running, get it out of your mind. You wouldn't travel fifty feet before I blasted you down."

MARK AND Mary sat in a small, cement-walled room in the basement of the Palmer House. A steel door had been put in. They were alone.

"Why are they waiting?" Mary asked.

"I don't know. Maybe they get a sadistic pleasure out of leaving us here together for a little while. It's hard to figure them."

"We tried, didn't we?"

"That we did. Are you scared?"

"No. Not as long as you're here. Does that sound corny?"

"It sounds wonderful."

They sat in silence for a long minute. Then Mark said, "It isn't over, of course. We'll get them in the end. But I guess you and I won't be around to see it."

"It doesn't matter too much. Others will take our places."

"It was a good fight though. That's the main thing. It was a good fight."

Mark leaned over and kissed Mary. Without passion— gently. But there was much in the kiss that was unspoken and understood.

Mark settled back into his place against the wall beside Mary. He took her hand. "No," he said. "It isn't over yet."

As a matter of fact, it seemed just to have started. At that moment the door flew open. Glan stood there with several *zants*—all armed—all alert—all very grim.

"Come on," Glan fairly shouted. "Things have been happening! We did the impossible! We smashed the ray-cap machines—four of them. It cost us twenty fighters, but then the natives came in."

Glan and the *zants* were rushing Mark and Mary up to street level. "And more than that," he said. "A whole army of natives came in under the water—under the ray-cap. Between us, we took the city!"

Mark's lips went tight. "Halley—the little native who used to come in and out—the one who brought me here—where is he?"

Above—in the hallway—a gun flared at that precise moment. Two of the *zants* went down, their crumpled bodies half burned away. "Here I am, Clayton," Halley blazed. There was a gun gripped tightly in his hand, and madness in his eyes. "We haven't failed! You'll never beat us! We haven't failed!"

The last words came as an echo from charred and blackened lips in a face that was falling into dust. Halley was dead.

"Let's go," Mark shouted. "Let's get going! Give me one of those guns."

But there was nothing to do. It was over—finished. And everyone knew Sargo and his proposed alliance was over, also. Within twenty-four hours, he was dead at the hands of his own people, and the eastern tiger crawled, snarling, back into its lair.

NOW EVENTS moved swiftly. The *zants*, now in command of their own destiny, yearned for the void. In a few hours, with no announcement whatever, they began boarding their ferries to reach the great ship.

Mark and Mary stood by the water's edge, having come there quickly as the news of the exodus spread. Mark turned to speak to Mary just as the latter jerked her hand from his. "The girl in Washington—" Mark began with concern. "There hasn't been time to—"

Mary was staring at him in blank surprise...

MARA STARED for several seconds at the strange, pale native who had been holding her hand. He seemed deeply surprised about something. "Mary!" the native said. "What's wrong?"

Mara continued to stare. Horror suddenly dawned in the native's face. "The scanner!" he mouthed. "The scanner! It's gone off!"

Mara wondered what he was talking about. She drew away from him and saw Glan running toward her. She smiled, and when Glan got there she ran into his arms.

"Mary! Mary!" the native cried, and Mara drew away from him.

Glan was smiling. "We're going back into the void," he said. "We're going to find a world that isn't inhabited. Isn't it wonderful?"

"Wonderful," Mara returned, laying her head on his shoulder.

The native seemed to be going mad. He took her by the arm and tried to drag her away from Glan. She laughed, so high were her spirits, and jerked free. She ran to the ferry, calling Glan after her, and they stepped into the ferry.

The gate closed and the ferry shot across the water toward the *Narkus*.

The native on the shore had completely lost his mind now. He stood there screaming after her at the top of his voice.

Mara watched him for a few moments, puzzled. Then she turned to listen to what Glan was saying, to listen to Glan tell her about the future.

She forgot the native until they were far up in void. Then she glanced down through a port.

All she saw was a small green ball—far away...

THE END

If you've enjoyed this book, you will not want to miss these terrific titles…

ARMCHAIR SCI-FI, FANTASY, & HORROR DOUBLE NOVELS, $12.95 each

D-1   **THE GALAXY RAIDERS** by William P. McGivern
SPACE STATION #1 by Frank Belknap Long

D-2   **THE PROGRAMMED PEOPLE** by Jack Sharkey
SLAVES OF THE CRYSTAL BRAIN by William Carter Sawtelle

D-3   **YOU'RE ALL ALONE** by Fritz Leiber
THE LIQUID MAN by Bernard C. Gilford

D-4   **CITADEL OF THE STAR LORDS** by Edmund Hamilton
VOYAGE TO ETERNITY by Milton Lesser

D-5   **IRON MEN OF VENUS** by Don Wilcox
THE MAN WITH ABSOLUTE MOTION by Noel Loomis

D-6   **WHO SOWS THE WIND…** by Rog Phillips
THE PUZZLE PLANET by Robert A. W. Lowndes

D-7   **PLANET OF DREAD** by Murray Leinster
TWICE UPON A TIME by Charles L. Fontenay

D-8   **THE TERROR OUT OF SPACE** by Dwight V. Swain
QUEST OF THE GOLDEN APE by Ivar Jorgensen and Adam Chase

D-9   **SECRET OF MARRACOTT DEEP** by Henry Slesar
PAWN OF THE BLACK FLEET by Mark Clifton.

D-10   **BEYOND THE RINGS OF SATURN** by Robert Moore Williams
A MAN OBSESSED by Alan E. Nourse

ARMCHAIR SCIENCE FICTION CLASSICS, $12.95 each

C-1   **THE GREEN MAN**
by Harold M. Sherman

C-2   **A TRACE OF MEMORY**
By Keith Laumer

C-3   **INTO PLUTONIAN DEPTHS**
by Stanton A. Coblentz

ARMCHAIR MASTERS OF SCIENCE FICTION SERIES, $16.95 each

M-1   **MASTERS OF SCIENCE FICTION, Vol. One**
Bryce Walton—"Dark of the Moon" and other tales

M-2   **MASTERS OF SCIENCE FICTION, Vol. Two**
Jerome Bixby—"One Way Street" and other tales

If you've enjoyed this book, you will not want to miss these terrific titles...

ARMCHAIR SCI-FI & HORROR DOUBLE NOVELS, $12.95 each

D-11 **PERIL OF THE STARMEN** by Kris Neville
THE STRANGE INVASION by Murray Leinster

D-12 **THE STAR LORD** by Boyd Ellanby
CAPTIVES OF THE FLAME by Samuel R. Delany

D-13 **MEN OF THE MORNING STAR** by Edmund Hamilton
PLANET FOR PLUNDER by Hal Clement and Sam Merwin, Jr.

D-14 **ICE CITY OF THE GORGON** by Chester S. Geier and Richard Shaver
WHEN THE WORLD TOTTERED by Lester del Rey

D-15 **WORLDS WITHOUT END** by Clifford D. Simak
THE LAVENDER VINE OF DEATH by Don Wilcox

D-16 **SHADOW ON THE MOON** by Joe Gibson
ARMAGEDDON EARTH by Geoff St. Reynard

D-17 **THE GIRL WHO LOVED DEATH** by Paul W. Fairman
SLAVE PLANET by Laurence M. Janifer

D-18 **SECOND CHANCE** by J. F. Bone
MISSION TO A DISTANT STAR by Frank Belknap Long

D-19 **THE SYNDIC** by C. M. Kornbluth
FLIGHT TO FOREVER by Poul Anderson

D-20 **SOMEWHERE I'LL FIND YOU** by Milton Lesser
THE TIME ARMADA by Fox B. Holden

ARMCHAIR SCIENCE FICTION CLASSICS, $12.95 each

C-4 **CORPUS EARTHLING**
by Louis Charbonneau

C-5 **THE TIME DISSOLVER**
by Jerry Sohl

C-6 **WEST OF THE SUN**
by Edgar Pangborn

ARMCHAIR SCIENCE FICTION & HORROR GEMS SERIES, $12.95 each

G-1 **SCIENCE FICTION GEMS, Vol. One**
Isaac Asimov and others

G-2 **HORROR GEMS, Vol. One**
Carl Jacobi and others

If you've enjoyed this book, you will not want to miss these terrific titles…

ARMCHAIR SCI-FI, FANTASY, & HORROR DOUBLE NOVELS, $12.95 each

D-21   **EMPIRE OF EVIL** by Robert Arnette
          THE SIGN OF THE TIGER by Alan E. Nourse & J. A. Meyer

D-22   **OPERATION SQUARE PEG** by Frank Belknap Long
          ENCHANTRESS OF VENUS by Leigh Brackett

D-23   **THE LIFE WATCH** by Lester del Rey
          CREATURES OF THE ABYSS by Murray Leinster

D-24   **LEGION OF LAZARUS** by Edmond Hamilton
          STAR HUNTER by Andre Norton

D-25   **EMPIRE OF WOMEN** by John Fletcher
          ONE OF OUR CITIES IS MISSING by Irving Cox

D-26   **THE WRONG SIDE OF PARADISE** by Raymond F. Jones
          THE INVOLUNTARY IMMORTALS by Rog Phillips

D-27   **EARTH QUARTER** by Damon Knight
          ENVOY TO NEW WORLDS by Keith Laumer

D-28   **SLAVES TO THE METAL HORDE** by Milton Lesser
          HUNTERS OUT OF TIME by Joseph E. Kelleam

D-29   **RX JUPITER SAVE US** by Ward Moore
          BEWARE THE USURPERS by Geoff St. Reynard

D-30   **SECRET OF THE SERPENT** by Don Wilcox
          CRUSADE ACROSS THE VOID by Dwight V. Swain

ARMCHAIR SCIENCE FICTION CLASSICS, $12.95 each

C-7   **THE SHAVER MYSTERY, Book One**
       by Richard S. Shaver

C-8   **THE SHAVER MYSTERY, Book Two**
       by Richard S. Shaver

C-9   **MURDER IN SPACE**
       by David V. Reed

ARMCHAIR MASTERS OF SCIENCE FICTION SERIES, $16.95 each

M-3   **MASTERS OF SCIENCE FICTION, Vol. Three**
       Robert Sheckley, "The Perfect Woman" and other tales

M-4   **MASTERS OF SCIENCE FICTION, Vol. Four**
       Mack Reynolds, Part One, "Stowaway" and other tales

If you've enjoyed this book, you will not want to miss these terrific titles…

ARMCHAIR SCI-FI & HORROR DOUBLE NOVELS, $12.95 each

D-31 **A HOAX IN TIME** by Keith Laumer
INSIDE EARTH by Poul Anderson

D-32 **TERROR STATION** by Dwight V. Swain
THE WEAPON FROM ETERNITY by Dwight V. Swain

D-33 **THE SHIP FROM INFINITY** by Edmond Hamilton
TAKEOFF by C. M. Kornbluth

D-34 **THE METAL DOOM** by David H. Keller
TWELVE TIMES ZERO by Howard Browne

D-35 **HUNTERS OUT OF SPACE** by Joseph Kelleam
INVASION FROM THE DEEP by Paul W. Fairman,

D-36 **THE BEES OF DEATH** by Robert Moore Williams
A PLAGUE OF PYTHONS by Frederick Pohl

D-37 **THE LORDS OF QUARMALL** by Fritz Leiber and Harry Fischer
BEACON TO ELSEWHERE by James H. Schmitz

D-38 **BEYOND PLUTO** by John S. Campbell
ARTERY OF FIRE by Thomas N. Scortia

D-39 **SPECIAL DELIVERY** by Kris Neville
NO TIME FOR TOFFEE by Charles F. Meyers

D-40 **JUNGLE IN THE SKY** by Milton Lesser
RECALLED TO LIFE by Robert Silverberg

ARMCHAIR SCIENCE FICTION CLASSICS, $12.95 each

C-10 **MARS IS MY DESTINATION**
by Frank Belknap Long

C-11 **SPACE PLAGUE**
by George O. Smith

C-12 **SO SHALL YE REAP**
by Rog Phillips

ARMCHAIR SCIENCE FICTION & HORROR GEMS SERIES, $12.95 each

G-3 **SCIENCE FICTION GEMS, Vol. Two**
James Blish and others

G-4 **HORROR GEMS, Vol. Two**
Joseph Payne Brennan and others